This month, in

THE MILLIONAIRE'S PREGNANT BRIDE
by Dixie Browning,

Meet William Bradford—CFO of Wescott Oil and
millionaire cowboy. His marriage to the lovely
Diana Foster was supposed to be in name only.
But it wasn't long before Will found himself
wishing Diana would be his wife…in every way!

**SILHOUETTE DESIRE
IS PROUD TO PRESENT THE**

**Five wealthy Texas bachelors—all members of
the state's most exclusive club—set out to
uncover the traitor in their midst…
and find true love.**

* * *

**And don't miss
HER LONE STAR PROTECTOR
by Peggy Moreland,
the second installment of the**
Texas Cattleman's Club: The Last Bachelor series.
Available next month in Silhouette Desire!

Dear Reader,

Escape the winter doldrums by reading six new passionate, powerful and provocative romances from Silhouette Desire!

Start with our MAN OF THE MONTH, *The Playboy Sheikh*, the latest SONS OF THE DESERT love story by bestselling author Alexandra Sellers. Also thrilling is the second title in our yearlong continuity series DYNASTIES: THE CONNELLYS. In *Maternally Yours* by Kathie DeNosky, a pleasure-seeking tycoon falls for a soon-to-be mom.

All you readers who've requested more titles in Cait London's beloved TALLCHIEFS miniseries will delight in her smoldering *Tallchief: The Hunter*. And more great news for our loyal Desire readers—a *brand-new* five-book series featuring THE TEXAS CATTLEMAN'S CLUB, subtitled THE LAST BACHELOR, launches this month. In *The Millionaire's Pregnant Bride* by Dixie Browning, passion erupts between an oil executive and secretary who marry for the sake of her unborn child.

A single-dad surgeon meets his match in *Dr. Desirable*, the second book of Kristi Gold's MARRYING AN M.D. miniseries. And Kate Little's *Tall, Dark & Cranky* is an enchanting contemporary version of *Beauty and the Beast*.

Indulge yourself with all six of these exhilarating love stories from Silhouette Desire!

Enjoy!

Joan Marlow Golan

Joan Marlow Golan
Senior Editor, Silhouette Desire

Please address questions and book requests to:
Silhouette Reader Service
U.S.: 3010 Walden Ave., P.O. Box 1325, Buffalo, NY 14269
Canadian: P.O. Box 609, Fort Erie, Ont. L2A 5X3

The Millionaire's Pregnant Bride
DIXIE BROWNING

Silhouette
Desire

Published by Silhouette Books
America's Publisher of Contemporary Romance

Special thanks and acknowledgment are given to
Dixie Browning for her contribution to the
TEXAS CATTLEMAN'S CLUB:
THE LAST BACHELOR series.

SILHOUETTE BOOKS

ISBN 0-373-76420-0

THE MILLIONAIRE'S PREGNANT BRIDE

Visit Silhouette at www.eHarlequin.com

Printed in U.S.A.

DIXIE BROWNING

is an award-winning painter and writer, mother and grandmother. Her father was a big-league baseball player, her grandfather a sea captain. In addition to her nearly 80 contemporary romances, Dixie and her sister, Mary Williams, have written more than a dozen historical romances under the name Bronwyn Williams. Contact Dixie at www.dixiebrowning.com or at P.O. Box 1389, Buxton, NC 27920.

"What's Happening in Royal?"

NEWS FLASH, February—Word has it that one of Royal's sexiest tycoons has gone and gotten himself hitched—in a hurry! William Bradford has been the talk of the town since he and Diana Foster said "I do." Not much is known about the blushing bride, but she must be something special to have persuaded Will to give up his confirmed bachelor status! Several eyewitnesses report that Diana has a certain glow about her…could there already be a little Bradford on the way?

Also in the news, it looks like there might be trouble brewing at Wescott Oil. Rumors of missing money abound.... Is there a thief at large? Nobody seems to know for certain, but Wescott's new CEO, Sebastian Wescott, has refused to comment on the situation, except to say that he is looking into matters....

And what's going on at Royal's Texas Cattleman's Club? It seems a few of Royal's sexiest bachelors have made a bet as to which one of them will be the last bachelor left standing. Gents, if you need any help on this one, we know a few local ladies who'd be willing to lend a hand....

One

Will Bradford switched off the lights in his tenth-floor office in the Wescott Building and debated whether or not to stop off at the Royal Diner for a bowl of chili on the way home. Too much trouble, he decided. After spending one more in a long string of eighteen-hour days trying to unravel the mess left behind by the unexpected death of his partner and one-time friend, Jack Wescott, he wasn't up to dealing with anything as complicated as a grease-stained menu. His three-day-a-week housekeeper would have left something in the freezer he could zap in the microwave.

That is, if he could stay awake long enough to eat.

You'd think the man had deliberately tried to scramble the books, Will mused tiredly as he reached for the coat of his rumpled, Western-cut suit, slung it over his left shoulder and headed for the elevator.

God knows, Jack Wescott had shaved a few corners over the years, but things were in worse shape than anyone had expected. A fanatic regarding privacy, Jack had essentially distrusted anything with a hard drive. Like most successful enterprises, Wescott Oil had a large computer division, yet Jack had insisted on keeping a hands-on set of paper files under lock and key.

Probably, Will mused, because he'd engaged in more than a few questionable business practices along the way to building his oil empire. Jack had been equally reckless in his personal life. Will had known about some of it and suspected more, even though the friendship that had begun more than fifteen years ago had cooled over the past few years.

Jack had been a womanizer, both before and after his marriage had ended. That sort of thing wasn't easy to keep hidden in a town like Royal, where gossip was a stock in trade. What had taken everyone by surprise, however, had been the sudden appearance of an illegitimate son shortly after Jack's death; Dorian Brady had turned up last month in Royal.

The resemblance between Dorian and Sebastian Wescott, Jack's legitimate son and heir, was striking enough that no one had doubted the relationship, even before it had been checked out. It seemed that when any of Jack's old flames got pregnant, he bought them a one-way ticket out of town. Evidently one of them had read about Jack's death and told her son, who figured it was time to call in a long-overdue debt.

As much as he hated the scandal for Sebastian's sake, Will couldn't blame the guy. If Dorian resented Jack's shabby treatment of him and his mother, he hid it well. Sebastian had accepted him to the extent of taking his half brother into his home and giving him a job in the computer division of Wescott Oil. Now Seb was pushing for Dorian's membership in the Texas Cattlemen's Club.

Will decided to reserve judgment.

Jack's secretary was another matter. The first time he'd seen her, she'd been backing out of the Royal Diner, talking to someone still inside. He'd held the door and waited patiently—tired, but not too tired to appreciate the view.

Not that she'd been advertising the view. Just the opposite, in fact. There'd been nothing at all outstanding in the tan-gray gabardine dress she'd been wearing. The color had a name: one of those colors with "au" in the middle. Mauve, taupe. He could never remember what it was. With her glossy, brown hair and delicate build, it had looked coolly elegant on a day when the temperature could frazzle the calmest nerves.

Two shapely young women passed by the diner licking ice cream cones. They were wearing tight jeans and skimpy, skin-tight tops. He'd barely spared them a glance.

"It's over next to the library, I think," the lady standing in the doorway was saying. "I've got several boxes to go, once I sort through them."

Nice hips. Slender build, rounded in just the right places. Gabardine was a surprisingly sexy fabric when it hung—as this did—over a shapely pair of hips, merely hinting at the surface beneath.

He must have sighed. Will knew he hadn't said anything, because what could he have said other than, "Would you please either come in or go out, lady? It's nearly three in the afternoon and I haven't had lunch.''

She turned—gasped—and wiped a three-scoop ice cream cone across his chest. "Oh, my— Oh, dear— I'm so sorry!''

Will backed up, staring blankly down at the mess she'd made of one of his favorite ties. "It's all right," he assured her. Then, when she began mopping the mess up with a handkerchief in one hand, the rapidly melting cone in the other, he said, "Look, it's really all right, okay? No harm done.''

No harm a dry cleaner couldn't take care of. Trouble was, he had that three-thirty meeting. He could either go home and change clothes or go inside and have a quick lunch.

"Oh, Lord, I can't believe—and I think I know you, too. That's even worse.''

He was edging away, wanting to escape before his shoes caught the rest of her melting chocolate ice cream. "No problem. It's all right." She looked as if she might burst into tears, which would be the last straw. He didn't know her. Might have seen her around town somewhere—she was the kind of woman a man wouldn't notice right off, but when he did, she'd be worth a second look.

Only not today. Not under these circumstances.

"Excuse me, I think I'll go drown myself.''

Sticky, hot, irritated, he managed a smile. "Swimming pools frown on that sort of thing.''

"Is there still a French Foreign Legion? Do they take women? Look, I'm really, really—''

"Don't say it. Better go back inside and wash your hands before you get into more trouble.''

She opened her mouth, closed it again and sighed.

Looking disgustedly at the melting mess in her left hand, she tossed it in the trash receptacle, sighed again and walked away.

For several minutes Will stared after her. She was worth watching. Again, nothing particularly outstanding—no twitchy little behind, no slinky movements, she simply walked. Where the devil, he wondered, had he seen her before? There was something about her...

The second time he saw her was several days after the ice-cream episode. She was just coming out of the secretarial pool. On his way to meet someone in the lobby, he'd stopped and stared, tempted to go and ask her name and if she worked there and whether or not she'd be interested in exploring a brief, nonbinding relationship with him. Fortunately, she hadn't noticed. Fortunately, no one else had, either.

Equally fortunately, common sense had kicked in before he could be accused of workplace harassment. The trouble was, his social life had been moderated along with just about everything else as he'd neared the four-oh mark. He was out of practice.

He had seen her several times after that, and the less she did to call attention to her sexuality, the more intrigued he became. There was something challenging about a woman who went out of her way to downplay her feminine attractions. Made a man wonder what was under all the muted colors and understated styles. The lady was a challenge, and if there was one thing Will thrived on, it was challenge.

But not this kind of challenge.

He told himself it was probably something simple—maybe a minor midlife crisis. He'd made a policy of never mixing business with pleasure. In today's litigious society, it simply wasn't worth the risk of future embarrassment, awkwardness or worse. Even so, he'd been almost at the point of breaking his own rule and asking her out when Jack had moved in and staked a claim by whisking her up to the executive floor as his personal secretary.

Jack's tastes had invariably run to leggy blondes in thigh-high skirts, with big boobs and big blond hair. The Foster woman was a marked improvement. Quelling his own disappointment, Will had gone out three nights in a row with three different women and—always the gentleman—had managed to conceal his boredom.

As for what Diana Foster had seen in Jack Wescott, that was easy. At fifty-eight, the wealthy oilman had been in peak physical condition until he'd dropped dead of a massive heart attack. It was widely known that wealth was among the world's greatest aphrodisiacs, and Jack had been a practiced philanderer who enjoyed bragging about the notches on his bedpost.

At least he hadn't bragged about his latest conquest. If he had, Will might have decked the man. After which, Will would have been forced to sell his stock, turn in his resignation and move out to his ranch a few years earlier than he'd planned to retire.

What he couldn't understand now, after Jack's death, was what the quietly elegant Ms. Foster had gained from the affair. She still drove the same elderly sedan, still wore the same inexpensive classic styles and—so far as he could tell—owned no jewelry other than pearl studs and the type of wristwatch that could be purchased at most drugstores.

Not that he'd paid any particular attention to her, once he'd realized she was having an affair with his business partner. For all he knew, Jack might've been planning to marry the woman, even though Jack had sworn he would never let himself be trapped into marriage again.

But, if that had been the case, surely he'd have had his lawyers drawing up a prenuptial agreement, and there'd been nothing like that in the works when he'd died. As a rule, Jack had even his mistresses sign a settlement agreement so that they couldn't come back to haunt him. Dorian's mother had signed one, but obviously Dorian didn't consider the terms of the agreement to apply to him.

Waiting for the elevator, Will stroked the back of his neck, massaging away the tension that always seemed to settle there. Jack's will, which had been read four days ago, had been simple and direct. Other than a few token gifts to his household staff, Sebastian had inherited everything the IRS didn't claim.

As executor of Jack's estate, Will was still trying to reconcile a few discrepancies in his personal accounts. Jack had been notoriously delinquent when it came to balancing his own checkbooks.

Nodding to the night security guard who let him out of the building, Will set off to walk the eleven blocks to his own apartment. Maybe fresh air would work a miracle. Maybe his headache would ease and the incomprehensible entries on Jack's personal check stubs would miraculously begin to make sense.

And maybe he would quit obsessing on the quiet, elegant beauty who had begun to crop up in more than a few of his dreams.

On the long walk home, Will mulled over a few

minor discrepancies he'd come across just today. While the business's financial records were in excellent condition, thanks largely to his own hand on the controls, Jack's personal affairs weren't quite so tidy. In building the empire that bore his name, he had stepped on more than a few toes, cut more than a few corners and no doubt had paid off his share of politicians and predatory women. Which might account for the unexplained drafts for tens of thousands of dollars in the past few months.

Poor guy. He'd been warned more than once to tone down his lifestyle. Will had often heard him joke about having a few wild chickens come home to roost. One of them, Dorian Brady, already had.

How many more would there be?

Urged by the board to take over as president, Will had declined the honor. With Jack gone, he was now the senior partner, but getting himself mired any deeper in corporate crap wasn't among his long-term plans for the future. Once he turned over his tenth-floor offices to the mandatory outside auditors, he would have to clear out Jack's tower office to prepare for the new regime. Which meant he was probably going to need the help of Jack's secretary. He didn't know whether to dread it or look forward to it. All he knew was that the woman affected him in a way no woman had in nearly twenty years.

Midlife crisis?

Yeah…probably. And dammit, he didn't have time for it now.

Shoulders hunched, the tall, lean Texan strode along the empty sidewalk. This time of night, traffic was light. The weather was unusually mild for February despite the wind and the threat of rain. If he finished up by Friday, maybe he could spend a couple of days out at the ranch.

Or maybe not. There was still a lot of sludge to wade through before the company could move ahead at full speed. For a business the size of Wescott Oil to be run like a mom and pop market was not only criminal, it was damn near impossible in this age of government regulations and demanding stockholders. But by bribing and threatening the right people, Jack had managed to do things his way right up to the end.

The end...

God, what a waste. At fifty-eight, he'd looked no older than Will himself did at forty-one, thanks to great tailor, a good barber, a personal trainer and a top-notch plastic surgeon. For a man who routinely managed to tick off half of the Texas legislature and buy off the rest, he'd been one hell of a guy. He was going to be missed.

While a scratchy recording of Fleetwood Mac flowed from a battered portable phonograph, Diana propped a bare foot up on her lap and carefully painted her big toenail a deep shade of coral. Tears ran a crooked trail down her face, not because she missed Jack, exactly, but because...

Well, because it was such a waste. Underneath his crazy suspicions and his domineering ways, he'd been a good man. In some ways. At least he'd been good to her when it mattered most. Her mother had had the very best care right up to the end, and if it meant giving herself—Diana refused to call it selling herself—to a man like Jack Wescott, then it was well worth the shame.

Or the guilt. Whatever she was feeling, it probably wasn't grief, which was even more of a reason to feel guilty.

She screwed the cap on the bottle of nail polish, which she used only on her toes where it wouldn't show, and grabbed a tissue to blow her nose. "Get over it, Foster," she muttered. People said that all the time. Get over it. Deal with it.

And she would, she really would. She was nothing if not a realist. The thing was, she had never really wanted to be anyone's lover, especially having grown up in a household where love was never a factor.

Her parents had been what she'd once heard referred to as "tie-dyed rebels for peace." When the rebellion had lost its luster, her father had left his wife and daughter to "find himself." Lila, her mother, had gone to work in the cosmetics department of a local discount store for minimum wages and no benefits other than a minuscule discount.

Her father had eventually come back—still lost— and taken a job selling paper products. Less than a month later he had gotten drunk, blacked both his wife's eyes so she couldn't go to work, and then left town again.

They'd been "flower children." Their mottos: Make Love, Not War; If It Feels Good, Do It.

Growing up, Diana had rebelled against her parents' entire generation. Eventually she might have ended up marrying some nice, dull man, the antithesis of her own father. Someone who would have been good with children and kind to pets. Someone who would, at least, be there for his family.

Jack hadn't been a dull man, nor had he always

been nice. And while she'd let herself believe at first that he wanted to marry her, that had never been in the cards. He had set out on a deliberate campaign to seduce her, and once he'd discovered her weakness, he'd succeeded.

And now Jack was dead and she would soon be back in the secretarial pool. Jack's son Sebastian would be the new chairman, and Sebastian already had his own executive secretary, one who was more qualified for the position.

Diana's mother had never reconciled herself to the fact that her only child—her little princess—had settled for a secretarial course instead of trying for a college scholarship. "But, honey, you're so creative," she'd exclaimed so often in her fade-away voice.

"You mean because I used to write those awful poems for your birthday and Mother's Day? Mama, grow up. It's about time somebody in this family did."

That had been several years ago, before her mother had been diagnosed with cancer. Since then Diana had come a long way. She had found a job to help pay the bills and had ended up working for a man who had insisted on doing things in a way that would have probably driven most secretaries up the nearest wall. The system they'd worked out together had been somewhat unorthodox, but it had suited them both.

Well, she thought, sniffing and sighing heavily, that, too, was over. Done with. *Fini*. Period.

Period? Which reminded her of another possible problem....

But that was stress. Of course it was stress. They'd

always been careful—almost always. Although Jack, for all his polished charm, could occasionally be demanding, impatient and insensitive.

But it was over now, and she could get on with her life. Diana stretched her leg and wiggled her newly polished toes. Nail polish had been her favorite treat as a little girl. Her mother would polish her toenails and tell her it was because she was a princess, only she couldn't tell anyone. And they would look at each other and smile, and when her father came home, Diana would huddle in bed and listen to the awful fights and think, *I'm a secret princess. As soon as I'm big enough, Mama and I will go find our real home, and Daddy can't ever go there.*

Daddy had been killed when she was fourteen. By then she'd known she was no princess but only the daughter of a disillusioned flower child who lacked the courage to break away from her abusive marriage to an ex-hippy. Diana remembered her father chiefly for his long absences and his vicious temper.

"Girl, you are a mess! Get it together!" she growled softly to herself.

And she was going to, she really was. It would be awkward returning to the secretarial pool after months of working on the executive floor. For one thing it was a world-class rumor mill, and she herself would be the focus of an uncomfortable amount of gossip.

But before she made any decision she was going to have to help Mr. William K. Bradford, the senior partner and chief financial officer, sort out the mess Jack had left behind. And wouldn't you know, he'd turned out to be the man she'd plastered with melted chocolate ice cream.

Since then she'd tried to avoid him, hoping he would forget the incident, or at least forget who ruined what had to be a custom-tailored suit and a designer tie. Not to mention the white shirt. Chocolate stains were impossible to remove.

She could only hope he wouldn't remember her. He'd been wearing sunglasses. Maybe some of the ice cream had spattered those, too, and he hadn't seen her clearly.

The trouble was, she'd seen him. Had a good look at him, from his broad shoulders to his thick, dark hair and his wonderfully irregular features. What was there about certain men that made them so heart-breakingly attractive? There were probably thousands of men who were more handsome. Hundreds.

Dozens, at least. She didn't lose any sleep over any of them, while the very thought of having to work in close contact with Will Bradford was enough to make her break out in a heat rash. She hadn't exactly led a sheltered existence. She did know the facts of life. She simply didn't know how to deal with a man who made her think wicked thoughts so soon after her mother had died and she'd broken off with Jack.

So much for disapproving of her parents' early lifestyle. If It Feels Good, Do It.

She'd done it, and it hadn't even felt particularly good.

Huddling in the lopsided recliner her mother had bought at a going-out-of-business sale, she thought some more about William Bradford. He struck her as the kind of man who lived his life by a set of ironclad rules. She liked that in a man. Purpose. Discipline. Order.

From now on, Diana vowed, she would make rules of her own, rule number one being that she was in sole control of Diana Foster. From this day forward she would take complete responsibility for her own life.

Will was the last to arrive for the weekly dinner meeting in one of the smaller private rooms at the Texas Cattleman's Club, an exclusive establishment formed originally so that a few wealthy cattle barons and some of the early oilmen could escape from their wives for a night out. As years passed it had served as a convenient cover for a number of covert operations. Of the small group of close friends, all were ex-military and had been involved in any number of operations that never hit the news. Thank God things had been quiet on that front lately. With Jack's unexpected death, Will had had enough on his mind without having to fly off at a moment's notice to rescue some poor unfortunate who'd blundered into trouble.

Between missions, the club served as a fund-raising organization for various charities that had arisen as the small town of Royal doubled and tripled its size. Will was, unfortunately, a member of the club's committee whose duty it was to sift through the dozens of applications and choose a worthy recipient for the funds raised by the annual charity ball. He'd just as soon divide the take equally among the charities, but tradition precluded such a simple solution.

After nodding to a few of the older members dozing over their *Wall Street Journal*s in the cigar, brandy and wax-scented great room, Will opened the massive oak door and closed it quietly behind him. "Evening, gentleman," he greeted.

"Man, you look like hell." It was Jason, foreign advisor and CIA agent, the youngest of the group, who passed judgment on him.

Sebastian, Jack's son and newly appointed CEO of Wescott Oil, looked as though he hadn't slept in weeks. It was obvious his father's death and the new responsibilities had taken their toll. Gamely he grinned. "Things are that bad in your neck of the woods, huh?"

"Not bad. Shall we say...disorganized? If your father had suspected an OPEC spy of trying to infiltrate the company to gather information, he might have devised a similar plan for throwing him off track. Anyone ordered yet? What are we having?"

Their tastes were as varied as the men themselves. Keith Owens, owner of a computer software company, was still studying the bill of fare. Robert Cole, private detective with an old-money background, usually ordered seafood.

Will chose steak, medium rare, with a baked potato, no sour cream and a salad, which he didn't particularly want but which he ordered anyway because at his age a smart man started thinking about health and his own mortality.

Pity poor Jack hadn't started earlier.

Will hadn't had time to stop by the club in more than a week. Since every man present was the son, if not the grandson, of a former member, this group was the closest thing to family he was ever apt to have. He asked after each man individually, then took a sip of the single drink he allowed himself each evening and said, "Want to tell me what all the snickers were about when I walked in?"

"What snickers? Oh, you must mean the bet. Seb has the dubious honor of heading up this year's gala, and he suggested that since we're all aging bachelors, we place a bet on which one will still be standing alone by the end of the year. Whoever wins can have the consolation prize of choosing the beneficiary," Rob explained.

Will looked from one man to the other. "You're not serious. Hell, I outgrew that kind of thing in prep school."

Jason, the youngest member of the group, enjoyed his playboy reputation enough to pick up the challenge. "Not that I'm particularly interested in game playing—" he was widely known for his games with the fairer sex "—but I'll win this one in a walk-away."

"Pretty sure of yourself, aren't you, old boy?"

Jason, his eyes alight with amusement, said, "Yeah, that about covers it." It was widely known, as well, that Jason was allergic to marriage.

And while Will didn't particularly want to win the consolation prize, marriage was definitely not in his future. Once had been enough.

"So, that's settled," Sebastian said, sounding vastly relieved. "Lets me off the hook."

It occurred to Will that, under the circumstances, maybe one of the others should have taken over the task of heading up this year's shindig. It was a daunting task at the best of times, and the man had just lost his father, after all.

"Next item on the agenda," Keith Owens said

around a mouthful of stuffed quail. "What about Dorian? Do we invite him to join the club?"

Sebastian abstained from commenting. Caution urged Will to suggest they not make any hasty decisions, but before he could voice the thought, Jason spoke up. "I vote we sit on it for a few weeks. All due respect, Seb, but we don't really know this guy."

After a brief discussion, it was decided to postpone making a decision. Will was relieved. Jason had razor-sharp instincts. Will trusted his instinct on most matters. By the time his dessert of fresh fruit compote was served, he was too tired to enjoy it. Shoving it across the table, he said, "Sorry, fellows, but if I don't make it to bed in the next half hour, you'll have to scrape me up off the street. Been a hell of a week."

After handing the accounting books to the outside auditors, Will turned his full attention to Jack's messy personal records. Will had already learned two disturbing things. First, that Diana Foster lacked the required qualifications for the position she'd been given. Second, that aside from a nice raise, she'd been the recipient of several large sums of money deposited to a checking account soon after she'd been promoted to the position of Jack's executive secretary. Putting that together with a remark Jack had once made about Diana's mother being ill, Will came to a conclusion that had set his blood to boiling.

It wasn't the kind of thing he could come right out and ask: Did you sleep with Jack so that he would pay your mother's medical expenses? Hell, he didn't know her well enough to ask anything that personal. He wasn't sure he really wanted to know the answer.

Oh, yeah, and there was a third thing, too. He learned that Diana, in a pair of black slacks, bending over an open carton on the floor, had a sweetly rounded bottom that could make a marble statue salivate.

On the way up to the tower office, Will reminded himself that only a few months ago Jack's old secretary, Miss Lucy, had been put out to pasture, if not with a golden parachute, at least with a gold-plated umbrella. Shortly after that, Miss Foster had been yanked out of the secretarial pool and propelled upstairs to the executive suite.

Knowing the lady had sold herself to the highest bidder, Will felt slightly sick. She might not look the part, but she'd evidently become just one more in a long line of Jack's women.

What was she, vamp or virgin?

Obviously not the latter.

Which didn't change the fact that for the past few months, whenever they'd found themselves in the same elevator together he'd had to stare at the indicator buttons and think about something else. The ranch. His favorite horse. The chances of being trapped overnight in an elevator with Diana Foster.

None of which had helped. He had a feeling that in the pitch-dark depths of a West Virginia coal mine, he would be aware of her nearness. Aware that she had hair like a dark silk waterfall, eyes like melted chocolate and skin that looked cool as snow but hinted at banked fires underneath. If she wore perfume, it was not easily discernible. Instead there was an aura about her that reminded him of dark roses, satiny wood and fine wine.

Probably because he'd seen her on more than a few occasions in Jack's walnut-paneled offices.

It was Saturday morning. Will and Diana had both come in to clear out the last of the personal items in Jack's office so that the cleaning crew could do their job and Seb could call in the decorators. He managed to keep his mind on business for almost an hour until she turned, tape roller in hand, her dark hair brushing her shoulder. "Shall I label this box personal and put it with those others for Sebastian?"

"What's in it? Oh, yeah—trophies, certificates, pictures…" Jack with several politicians. Jack with a couple of Hollywood types. Jack with his foot on the neck of a dead lion, and another eight-by-ten glossy of Jack with a dead blue marlin. "Yeah, go ahead. Here, I'll move it for you."

"Use your knees, not your back," she warned in the voice that had come as something of a surprise the first time he'd ever heard it. Quiet, a little bit husky. The type of voice advertisers paid a fortune for, but without the fake seductiveness that was used to sell everything from potency pills to plumbing supplies.

"Huh?" Real intelligent, Bradford.

"To lift the box. Squat, don't just bend over. Better yet, drag it like I did all the others."

Will had a feeling Sebastian was going to want to change quite a few things now that he had the power. Father and son were nothing at all alike. They hadn't gotten along particularly well, although each was brilliant in his own way.

"Yes, ma'am," Will muttered, amused at Diana's

bossiness. Nevertheless, he bent his knees slightly, leaned over and lifted the box, which was filled with books, trophies and framed photographs. "Where?" he said with a grunt.

"There." She pointed.

He set it up on top of the stack by the door and managed to resist grabbing his back. Masking his grimace with a smile, he said, "I could do with some lunch, how about you?"

Turning slowly, Diana surveyed the spacious tower office with its paneled walls, the walnut louvered shutters and the heavy, lined linen draperies. Not for Jack Wescott the usual preference for glass, leather and steel.

"How much more do we have to do? I cleaned out the records room and the bathroom." A length of hair fell forward, and she brushed it back. That morning her heavy, straight brown hair had been confined in one of those twisted arrangements on the back of her head. He could have told her about hair like hers and the laws of gravity.

"Then that about does it," he said. "Cleaning staff will be in tonight. They can take down the curtains and either toss 'em or send 'em out to be cleaned. They've been here for as long as I can remember."

She touched the soft, sun-faded fabric the way a woman would. "I don't think Jack ever even noticed them. I guess most men wouldn't, but they're sort of nice, aren't they? In a subtle, understated kind of way."

"Yeah, I suppose so." So are you, lady. In a subtle, understated kind of way.

Will made up his mind to give her the draperies

once they came back from the cleaners. Unless her living quarters were a hell of a lot larger than his, he had no idea what she would do with all those yards of heavy, lined fabric. Slipcover her house, maybe.

Still, it eased his conscience, because as soon as they wound things up here, he'd already made up his mind to offer her a bonus and encourage her to leave town. The last thing poor Seb needed after dealing with the sudden death of his father and the appearance of an illegitimate half brother was to have to deal with any possible demands from his father's ex-mistress.

After washing up in the luxurious washroom, they locked the door and crossed the hall to the elevators. Dorian Brady and two clerks from the computer department got on at the floor below. Will nodded to Dorian. He was still withholding judgment when it came to Jack's by-blow. There was something about him—almost a watchfulness—that raised a few red flags.

But then, that was probably because Seb was Will's friend, and this guy, whatever his credentials, was an interloper.

As the elevator sped silently down to the lobby, Diana said, "What about the boxes of files I took home with me? Is there any hurry about going through them?"

The doors opened soundlessly, and the small group filed out but lingered nearby. Will, noticing the way Dorian was eyeing his late-father's secretary, moved to block his view as they crossed the plush lobby. If any man was going to ogle the woman, it wasn't going to be some shifty-eyed kid in a flashy two-toned suit and a bolo tie.

Not until they were outside did he answer her question. "It's all personal stuff, isn't it? Nothing to do with the estate?"

"The boxes? As far as I know."

"Then let's let it ride, okay? What do say we stop by the Royal for some chili and coconut pie?" He made the offer only because he'd kept her long past lunch time. All he really wanted to do was go home, watch headline news and sleep for the next twenty-four hours.

Well, maybe not all... "Or if you'd rather, we could drive over to Claire's."

And then, damned if she didn't start crying, right there in broad daylight.

Thank God the Saturday-morning traffic was light.

Well, hell...

Two

They ate at the Royal Diner. Diana ordered the chili and a glass of milk to douse the fire. She didn't talk much, but then, Will wasn't used to having conversation with his meals unless he ate at the club. He was still trying to figure out why she'd started crying, but when he'd asked her, she'd just shaken her head.

Women.

At least she'd stopped crying as suddenly as she'd started. Claimed dust had blown in her eye.

Sure it had.

"World-class coconut pie," he said, forking up the last bite from his plate. "Want to take a slice home with you—or maybe a whole pie?"

Another thing about her that got to him was her smile. It started with a crinkling of the eyes, tweaked the corners of her lips and then it was gone, almost making a man wonder if he'd only imagined it.

"No, but thank you. I'd better get home before the rain starts again. It doesn't rain often around here, but once it starts, it can make up for lost time."

"Weather's been crazy everywhere these past few years."

So Will drove her back to the office building and left her at her car. Earlier that morning he'd carried down a box of her personal belongings. A small box. Evidently, she traveled light. He'd found himself wondering what was in it. Her own personal photographs? Family? A boyfriend? He doubted that, under the circumstances.

He hardly knew her, but if he had to guess, he'd say she wasn't the type of woman to spread her personal relics around for public view.

But then, if he'd had to guess, he would never have pegged her for one of Jack's conquests, either.

When she started to close her car door, he held it open and leaned down. "You're sure you're all right, Diana? You look a little washed out."

"Thanks," she said, and shot him another one of her quirky smiles. "Nothing a little blusher won't take care of, I hope."

Will watched her as she drove away in an eighties model sedan that was just one of the mysteries about Diana Foster that plagued him. She had a face that could easily be called patrician. A body that was tall, almost too lean, yet definitely, temptingly feminine. She wore outfits that could be bought at any discount store, yet he could easily imagine her striding down a runway wearing one of those slinky, transparent, cut-down-to-here-and-up-to-there outfits designed to raise a man's blood pressure into the danger zone.

She could do that wearing black polyester slacks,

a cotton pullover sweater and a battered twill rain-
coat.

Watching her drive off, swerving to avoid the
deepest puddles, he visualized her mouth. She hadn't
bothered to replace the lipstick she'd eaten off with
her chili.

Because she'd forgotten?

Or because he wasn't worth the bother?

If she had any idea how vulnerable her naked lips
looked, she'd have layered it on with a roller.

Vulnerable?

Where the hell had that come from? Tack, his
ranch manager would have told him he'd been smoking too much locoweed.

One thing for sure—once the transition at work
was completed, he was going to hightail it out to the
ranch, spend a couple of weeks working with his
stock, and then maybe go fishing. Maybe Baja.
Maybe even the Outer Banks. Somewhere where nobody had ever heard of Wescott Oil.

It was still fairly early. Things were moving along
faster than she'd expected at the office, thanks to
Will Bradford's efficiency. The rest could probably
be accomplished in a few days. Mostly they had
worked on weekends, to avoid interference by curious staff members eager to see what changes would
be made, not only to the decor but to the operations.
Sebastian and his father had never seen eye-to-eye
on many things.

Pulling out of the employees' parking lot, Diana
imagined the big mug of cocoa she would have as
soon as she got home. Since earliest childhood it had
been her favorite comfort food, and, for no reason at

all, she felt in sudden need of comfort. Probably this crazy weather. The temperature had dropped since they'd left the diner. A gust of wind sent a plastic bag and a large paper cup, complete with lid and straw, scurrying across the street in front of her car, distracting her from her thoughts momentarily.

This was the kind of weather when she would like nothing better than to curl up with a good book and alternately read and doze for the next twelve hours.

She yawned. Stress again. Too many decisions to be made.

What she *should* do was go through those boxes Jack had sent home with her, as if he'd had some sort of premonition. For all she knew, they contained Sebastian's baby pictures and report cards. Or maybe love letters from all the women who had gone before her. She'd heard the whispers before she'd ever met the man.

But she was simply too tired tonight. Ever since Jack had died, two months ago, she'd been trying to make plans for the future. The trouble was she couldn't seem to stay awake long enough to eat, much less to decide whether or not to move back to the secretarial pool at Wescott or pack up, leave town and look for another job in a new town where she didn't know a soul.

Lately, all she seemed able to do was weep and sleep. Maybe she needed vitamins.

Without thinking, she pulled into the parking lot outside the small walk-in clinic she had passed every day on her way to work. There was probably nothing wrong with her that a handful of vitamins and a good night's sleep wouldn't cure, but why take chances? She needed to recover her energy if she was going to get through these next few days and decide on her future. Preventive medicine couldn't prevent everything, but she was still a firm believer in taking control. Of her health, her life—everything. It wouldn't hurt to have a professional check her out while she still had her company insurance, in case she decided to move on.

Little more than an hour later Diana walked out in a daze, oblivious to the rain that pounded down on her bare head. Oblivious to the wind that whipped her tan trench coat around her legs.

Pregnant?

Impossible!

Impossible but true. Three months, as far as Dr. Woodbury could determine without further tests. "Does it have to go on my record?" Diana had asked the nurse, thinking of all the embarrassing questions that could, and probably would, be asked. She didn't know how many people had guessed about her and Jack—they'd both gone out of their way to be discreet, but in a town like Royal, secrets had a way of leaking out.

"Not if you don't intend to use your insurance."

"Oh. Well, could I just pay cash today and think about it?" With any luck, she could be in another town, settled in another job before she needed further medical attention.

Was pregnancy considered a preexisting condition?

Diana had a feeling the nurse was good at reading between the lines. "We can work it out any way that suits you, hon. Stop by the window and you can either pay today or we'll bill you. Here, you'll want to read these pamphlets. They tell you what to expect at which stage. Right now it's one thing, tomorrow it might be something else. We'll make you an appointment for six weeks, shall we?''

Diana nodded, knowing she wouldn't be in Royal in another six weeks. This changed everything. Leaving was no longer an option, it was imperative. Once the pregnancy began to show and people put two and two together and realized whose baby she was carrying, things would be awkward, to say the least.

A baby.

To think she'd vowed to take control of her own life from here on out. Evidently, she hadn't made the decision soon enough. She had always tried to be careful, but there had been that one time…. Jack had never been known for his patience. One time was all it took.

Out on the sidewalk she took a deep breath and tried to quell the rising panic by reminding herself that she'd always been the most levelheaded member of her family. The *only* levelheaded member.

After her father had died, her mother had fallen apart. Blamed herself and wept endlessly, claiming she hadn't been a good enough wife. As much as she hated to admit it now, Diana had lost patience with her mother more than once. She had honestly thought, though, that if they moved to a new locale, her mother might perk up and take an interest in life again.

So they'd moved to Royal, Texas, a place she'd heard mentioned on the news one night, and she'd got a job as a secretary at Wescott Oil.

Instead of perking up, Lila Foster's depression had grown worse, until Diana had insisted she undergo a complete examination to rule out any physical cause for her lethargy. It was only then that her mother had been diagnosed with advanced ovarian cancer.

Frantic, Diana had been arguing with the insurance department at Wescott the day she'd met Jack Wescott, founder and chief shareholder of Wescott Oil.

"Whoa, little lady," he'd said, clasping her by the arms as she'd backed out the door, still yelling, just as he was entering the building. He had held her a moment too long, staring at her angry tears, then he'd asked her name.

A week later she'd been moved up to the executive floors, where Jack, who was old enough to be her father, had begun a determined assault on her heart.

At least, she'd thought at the time it was her heart. Frantic with worry, she'd made mistake after mistake. It was a wonder she hadn't been fired, but instead Jack had given her a raise and stepped up his courtship, offering her jewelry, a car, even a house.

It was when she'd burst into tears and poured out her story that he'd offered the one thing she hadn't been able to refuse. The finest care available for her mother.

By the time her mother had died, Diana had been spending her days at the hospital and at least three nights a week with Jack at his lake cabin. Numbly, she'd gone through the motions of sex, often crying before it was over.

If he'd been brutal, she could almost have borne it better, but instead he'd been tender. They hadn't been in love, but the relationship they'd shared had had value to him. She had an idea she was the only one who had realized it, but in his own way, Jack

had been as lonely as she was. She had broken it off
after her mother's death. He'd seemed to understand.

And now she was going to have his baby. Thank
goodness no one knew about it. The sooner she left
town, the better.

The next morning Diana lay in bed, trying to find
the energy to get up. She hadn't accomplished a single thing when she'd gotten home from the clinic the
day before. Instead she'd crashed on the miserable
sofa with a sprung spring stabbing her in the ribs.
She had slept, woken up and eaten half a box of
vanilla wafers and then slept some more. That night
she had lain awake for hours, trying to organize her
life into some workable pattern.

A baby. Dear Lord, she couldn't even manage to
make decisions for herself. How could she ever take
care of a baby?

By morning the rain had ended, but the temperature had plummeted still further. She crawled out of
bed shivering, thought about breakfast and decided
against it—too many vanilla wafers in the middle of
the night could do that to a woman. Instead she
dressed in her warmest slacks and a turtleneck
sweater and headed for the office. There was a certain security in habit. Time to start breaking old hab-
its and forming new ones, Diana reminded herself,
only not quite yet. Not today.

Now, eleven stories up in the tower office where
she'd worked for the past few months, Diana gazed
out the undraped windows, watching as men in over-
coats and wool-lined denim jackets moved briskly
along the sidewalks below. Limousines and pickup
trucks moved sedately along Royal's Main Street.

Women wearing fur coats and custom-made boots dashed from heated cars to heated churches.

Winter came in several varieties in Texas. Wet and cold was the worst. Silently she vowed that the next time she relocated, it would be to a place where the seasons were more temperate. She'd had enough of extremes.

Will, too, was leaning against a windowsill. He'd been there when she'd come in, and she'd apologized for no logical reason for being late. Neither of them had been obligated to come in today. There wasn't that much more to do.

"I don't know what's wrong with me." Well, she did, of course…. "I've always been a morning person."

"Not a problem. I wasn't expecting you, anyway. There's nothing much more to be done here."

The cleaning crew had already started. The curtains were gone, the carpet people would be in next. Diana was surprised that Will was there at all, but then, his own office was probably overrun with auditors.

"You're right." She sighed, marveling at how drastically life had changed for a little girl who had once depended on toenail polish for her identity.

Feeling his eyes on her, she glanced up, wondering at the fleeting expression of…what? Interest? She'd known for days that he was curious about her. The trouble was, she'd been just as curious—just as interested in him, even before that. What woman wouldn't be?

But anything more than the business relationship they had cautiously established was out of the question. If she'd learned one lesson it was the value of separating business from personal life. By now everyone must have guessed why the newest hired secretary in the pool had been yanked upstairs to work for the boss.

Will must certainly have guessed. Avoiding his look, she scuffed the toe of her loafers over an ink stain on the carpet under the edge of Jack's desk. "I hope the cleaners can get it out. But then, Sebastian…" She didn't know him personally, but for now there was only one Mr. Wescott at Wescott Oil, and that was still Jack. "He'll probably want to have the whole place recarpeted."

Ignoring her remark, Will said, "What would you say to transferring to the Houston offices?"

She felt behind her for a chair. As much as she'd been thinking about relocating—especially now that she knew about the baby—the one thing she hadn't considered was a transfer. "You mean go on working for Wescott Oil?"

He nodded. The way he was studying her made her wonder if she'd remembered to floss her teeth before she'd dashed out that morning. Lately she'd been feeling so awful it was all she could do to get out of bed. She still felt queasy, probably from skipping breakfast.

Or maybe not.

"You don't have any family here, as I understand it. No…close relationships?"

He *had* to have suspected what had been going on. The two men had been friends for years, according to Jack. Besides, as CFO, he must have known about the money Jack had given her to pay her mother's bills, even though she was almost certain it had come out of Jack's personal account.

Had Sebastian known?

How utterly embarrassing. Houston might not be far enough away if everyone in town knew about her relationship with the Wescott of Wescott Oil.

Sebastian and her baby would be half brothers. And half brother to the new man in the computer division, Dorian Brady. According to the grapevine, he'd been another of Jack's mistakes.

Diana took three deep, slow breaths. It didn't help. She swallowed a sudden surge of nausea. Things were getting entirely too complicated. If Sebastian had any idea she was pregnant with Jack's baby, would he try to take it away from her? *Could* he?

He was certainly in a better position to take care of a child than she was. Hadn't he taken in his illegitimate half brother, Dorian?

If she'd had to have an affair, why couldn't it have been with an ordinary man instead of a man who could reach out from the grave and steal her baby from her?

But, of course, an ordinary man would never have been able to do what Jack had done for her mother.

Will moved away from the window, flexing his broad shoulders. Even looking as if she'd swallowed a fly, the lady was a major distraction. "We've got everything under control here. Why don't you take off for a few days. Think over what I said about transferring to Houston and give me your answer next week, all right?"

He watched the last dregs of color fade from her face and wondered what the devil he'd said to cause her to look as if she'd lost her last friend in the world.

Suddenly she turned and rushed into the private bathroom Jack had recently had fitted out with a hot tub and a large screen TV. Sounds of retching came clearly through the door, which had bounced open when she'd slammed it behind her.

"Miss Foster? Diana? Are you okay?"

Come to think of it, she'd looked sort of shaky every morning they'd worked together. No matter what she'd said about being a morning person, some women simply weren't at their best early in the day.

She was on her knees, struggling to get to her feet when he let himself in. "Diana? Look, if you need to go home, I'll drive you, all right? You're obviously in no shape to drive yourself."

She turned to him then. Big brown eyes, looking like chestnuts in the snow. "Yes, I am," she said, swallowing hard. "I'm just fine."

Will dampened a towel and handed it to her, and she held it to her face for a moment. A long moment. He was still standing there, feeling acutely uncomfortable, when she looked up at him again.

"If I transfer to Houston, I'd still have my company insurance, wouldn't I?"

"Insurance? Yeah, sure. Want to tell me why that's so important?"

She stared at him, abject misery in every line of her slender body, and the answer suddenly blindsided him. "Oh, hell! You're pregnant, aren't you?"

To her credit, she didn't try to lie. "Just barely."

"Just barely? Just a *little bit* pregnant?"

"Look, it's not a problem. I mean, I can go on working for months once my hormones settle down, according to—well, the experts."

"And which experts would that be?"

She shook her head, reached behind her to put down the lid, then sat on the commode. Will sat on the edge of the monstrous hot tub with the gold-plated faucets and the mini refrigerator within easy reach. He wondered if Diana and Jack had ever used it together.

"It doesn't matter. It doesn't concern you or Wescott Oil or anyone else but me. I paid cash at the clinic. And Houston's fine. How soon can I transfer?"

"Whoa, hang on a minute. This changes things."

"No, it doesn't."

She was making an effort to conceal it, but the lady was scared out of her penny loafers. She was shivering, and the temperature was somewhere in the low seventies.

"Hot tea? Isn't that the usual prescription? I'll make some tea and see if I can find some crackers."

"No, that's…" Her voice trailed off, and she nodded weakly. "A cola? Something carbonated?"

So he led her back into the office and settled her in the most comfortable chair. She looked lost. Vulnerable. He didn't think she'd appreciate being told as much, so he poured a freshly opened soda over ice and waited for it to fizz down while he thought of the best course of action.

Under the circumstances there was no best course of action. All the same, he knew what he had to do.

"Is it Jack's?" He was pretty sure it was, but he was a firm believer in covering all the bases.

"That doesn't concern you." She met his eyes with a miserable but unwavering look that was sheer bravado.

The baby was Jack's. Otherwise, she would have denied it. He'd come to recognize a basic honesty about the woman in the brief time they'd been working together. It was just one of too many things about her that drove him a little crazy. One minute he'd be thinking of her as just another in a long line of Jack's women. The next, he'd be looking at her as the innocent victim of a lecherous jerk who knew exactly which button to push when he wanted something.

Or someone.

For years Will had been dealing with the untidy loose ends left by his hardheaded, heedless friend. Ladies who claimed Jack had promised to marry them, when Will knew damned well the man had never promised any such thing. Jack had been married once, to Sebastian's mother. That had been before Will's time. Will hadn't asked about it, and Jack had never volunteered any information. Neither had Sebastian.

As for his long string of alliances, most lasting no more than a few months, Jack usually made the women sign releases before he even took them to bed. He hadn't gotten where he was by being careless about minor details.

One woman claimed he'd given her a house in Midland but had forgotten to give over the deed. Jack had been dead only three days when she'd come barreling up to the top floor to demand that deed.

Will, still in shock himself, had taken the time to look into the matter and discovered that his reckless friend had given her a one-year lease on a tract house. As the lease still had seven months to run, he'd let it stand.

No woman, to his knowledge, had ever come forth claiming to be pregnant with a little Wescott heir, though it was possible that more than one had found herself in that condition. As a rule Jack paid his women off and hustled them out of town if there was the slightest possibility of that happening.

Matter of fact, this woman hadn't made the claim, either. Which was only one of the reasons why Will decided to clean up one last mess his untidy friend had left behind. He wasn't sure Diana could handle it financially—knew damned well she couldn't handle it emotionally if today was an example.

"Feeling better now? Look, don't worry about the insurance. If I set the wheels in motion right away, we can be married within the week."

Her jaw fell. It was a delicate jaw, one he'd like to cup with his hand, but this was hardly the time. "I'm talking a business arrangement, Diana. I have a pretty good idea of your resources—" At her look of indignation, he said, "Yeah, I know, I had no right, but you see, one of the trails I had to follow to unravel Jack's financial affairs led directly to your bank account. I finally figured it out with a little research." Not to mention recalling a few of Jack's insensitive remarks that Will had only recently put into context.

She was breathing too fast. There was an angry spark in her eyes that he'd as soon not have to deal with. But determined to settle things before she split, he plowed ahead.

"Look, it makes sense as a purely business arrangement. I'm unattached. You're unattached. You need something that I can offer."

"Fine." She crossed her arms over her chest— breasts. Uh-uh, he preferred to think of the area as a chest. "What do you need, Mr. Bradford? That is, what would you get out of it?"

His smile held little warmth. "Call me Will...Danny."

"My name is Diana," she snapped icily.

"Right. Diana. As for what I need, how about that warm feeling you get when you write a check to your favorite charity?"

Oops. Another misstep. Switching gears, he leaned his hips against the windowsill and tried to reason with her from another direction. "I take it Jack didn't ask you to sign an agreement?" At her look of confusion, he nodded. "I thought not. By paying your mother's hospital bills he had you right where he wanted you. But you see, Jack's gone now. You're going to need some help and I don't want Sebastian to be—"

"As if I would go to Sebastian! This is none of his business—nor yours, either!"

"Are you going to keep it?"

"My baby? Of course I'm going to keep it, it's mine!" Her hands went to her stomach, still flat and almost too lean.

Will read her thoughts as clearly as if she'd spoken them. In a few months—maybe even a few weeks—it wouldn't be quite so flat. There was bound to be talk, even if she transferred to Houston. Hell, half the folks in Texas knew Jack's reputation. All it would take was a few words, and poor Seb would find himself saddled with another of his father's by-blows. Whether or not she agreed, Seb's conscience would make him step in.

"Look, if we get married, there are several ways we can handle this. We can settle on a lump sum—enough to support you and the baby until you can get back on your feet, or we can—"

"Absolutely not!" Her eyes sparkled angrily.

"Or I could lease you a place to live and arrange for a monthly stipend to be paid into an account. Of course, you'd have to sign a release, but we can work that out later."

He wondered if she was going to take a swing at him. In all honesty he couldn't much blame her if she did. It was a hell of a position to be in, having to insult a woman to make sure she was taken care of. "You don't have to decide right this minute."

"Fine. I'll let you know in a few years what you can do with your generous offer."

Ouch. How the hell did a man handle a pregnant female porcupine? It wasn't as if he was interested in her personally.

At least, not seriously. That wouldn't even make sense.

"I'm talking about a business arrangement. Think about it and I'll call you in the morning."

Five minutes after Will left, Diana was sitting where he had left her, staring at a tiny dark spot on the cream carpet where one of Jack's cigar ashes had fallen. Jack had been rough on carpets.

On women, too, she thought sadly.

As for Will, he was out of his mind. Did he really think she was that desperate? If there was one thing she had learned early in life it was that a bad marriage was not the answer to anyone's problems. No child of hers was going to grow up the way she had, hiding her head under the covers, telling herself that any day now a kindly king would see the polish on her toenails and recognize her as his long-lost daughter.

A business arrangement. Ha!

First thing in the morning she would call personnel and see if she could set the transfer into motion herself.

One floor below, Will sat in his own quiet office, both feet propped on his desk, and stared at the single painting on his wall. It was one he'd commissioned of the modest ranch he'd bought soon after he'd gone to work for Jack Wescott. He'd had nothing particular in mind when he'd bought the place—a few thousand acres of woods and grassland, with a farmhouse and a few outbuildings. Since then he had built himself a house and hired a couple to stay in the old house and look after things. He'd simply needed something more than his job. A bolt hole, in case Jack ever went too far over the line and things blew up.

It hadn't happened. Jack had managed to stay just this side of the law, including the countless miles of red tape that all but hamstrung the oil industry. Will had become a full partner, and the ranch had become a place to unwind when he could spare the time. He had a small herd of quarter horses, good breeding stock. Tack Gilbert, his manager, had hired a few hands to look after the place. Diana could stay there until the baby was born, and then they could renegotiate.

At least he'd do better by her than Jack had done by Dorian's mother. Whoever the poor woman had been, she'd probably deserved better than being handed a one-way ticket out of town.

Will had no interest in marrying again, in spite of that damn fool bet the guys had made the other night at the club. He'd never forgiven himself for not being there when Shelly, his wife, had been killed.

But in this case, marriage was the simplest solution. He could marry Diana, claim the baby as his own and spare poor Seb from any more unpleasant revelations. Whether or not anyone believed him, they'd have better sense than to question his claim. He and Diana could spend the occasional weekend together for the sake of appearances, then, after a year or so, they could renegotiate.

Hell, even that much was better than a lot of the marriages he knew about. Half the men his age had been married and divorced at least once.

He happened to know Diana's age. She was twenty-eight to his forty-one. An uncomfortable stretch if this were to be a normal marriage, but it wasn't. She was carrying another man's baby and as for him, lust notwithstanding, he was long past the age for romance.

"Ah, Jack, you sorry son of a gun," he muttered. "You're not worth the salt it would take to cure your hide. I'm doing this for your kid's sake, not yours."

Maybe he was, and maybe he was doing it for another reason, one he'd as soon not examine too closely.

Hell, it was the right thing to do, and so he'd do it.

Three

Diana dressed carefully in a black three-piece suit with a gray silk blouse, examined her image in the mirror, then quickly removed the outfit and tossed it on the pile on her bed.

Smile, for heaven's sake, you're getting married today!

The softest, most romantic thing she owned was a muumuu or her peach-colored sweatsuit. Hardly wedding wear, she thought ruefully.

It was a business arrangement, strictly, and only that, she reminded herself. She had called Will on the private number he'd given her and had said, "Yes. All right, I will." Just that, no more. Then she'd congratulated herself on taking control of her life and doing what was best for her baby.

Will had set the time and place with no more interest in his voice than if he'd been scheduling a routine visit to the dentist. He would probably wear the same thing he wore to work every day—one of those stunning suits that whispered "Texas" without all the fancy piping and waist-hugging style so many men seemed to go for.

By all rights, she should wear the same kind of thing she'd worn every day to the office. Something that wouldn't demand attention, that wouldn't have to be dry-cleaned after each wearing and something that could in no way be described as seductive. Something suitably secretarial.

One look at her apartment reminded her of why she dressed the way she did—in tailored suits, shirt-waist dresses in conservative colors and sensible shoes.

"Oh, Mama, you really did a number on me, didn't you?" she whispered, picking up one of Lila's beloved candles, the scented wax embedded with seashells. Her mother's touch was everywhere, from the lava lamps and beaded macramé wall hangings to the lavender walls and orange shag rug. Hoping to pull her out of her depression when they'd moved to Royal, Diana had encouraged Lila to decorate their small apartment, claiming she was too busy settling into her new job.

The result had turned out to be a colorful cross between early thrift shop and late Woodstock, but Diana hadn't complained—she'd hardly noticed. With settling into a new job in a new town and worrying about her mother's increasing listlessness, a tacky apartment had been the least of her concerns. She had lived in far worse places.

Then her mother's condition had been diagnosed. After that, the apartment had served only as a place where she kept her clothes so that she could rush in and change between work and the hospital.

And Jack's cabin....

Now, without ever having come to terms with the past, she was about to take on the role of Mrs. William Bradford. A *temporary* role, she told herself. Just until the baby came and she was settled in a new job, a new town. It might seem as if she was relinquishing control over her life, but she wasn't. Not really. She was only being sensible. The best insurance she could have was that her baby would be born a Bradford. Without DNA testing, which she would refuse to permit, no one could prove otherwise. At the very least it should settle any perceived risk of her cashing in on Jack's name.

"I'll make sure to lay in a good supply of nail polish, honey pie," she murmured, touching the place where only inches away, her daughter or son lay sleeping.

What if it was a boy? She could hardly polish his toenails and offer him hope by telling him he was a secret prince. Maybe she could afford to buy him a pony. What little boy wouldn't love to grow up to be a cowboy?

The wedding was to take place in Judge Shirley Mattock's offices on Friday afternoon at four. The guests consisted of Will's closest friends, Sebastian Wescott, Jason Windover, Keith Owens and Robert Cole. She had met Sebastian, of course, at work. The others were strangers.

Why hadn't she thought to invite someone of her own?

Not that she had any close friends in Royal. There hadn't really been time to make friends before she'd been plucked out of the secretarial pool and sent up to the tower office. After that, the other women she'd worked with had seemed rather cool.

Don't you dare get sick, she warned herself silently, quelling a familiar uneasy feeling. Will had insisted on picking her up, but she'd insisted right back. "It's unlucky for the groom to see the bride on her wedding day," she'd told him. "I'll drive."

She pulled in to the parking lot behind the courthouse only five minutes later. Will was there to meet her. "I was afraid you'd changed your mind and skipped town."

"I can still do that," she told him. "It's not too late to withdraw your offer." So much for that old superstition about the bride and groom not seeing each other before the ceremony on the day of the wedding. Maybe it didn't count, since it wasn't that kind of a wedding.

"We had an agreement. I don't go back on my word." He leveled a piercing stare at her and asked, "Do you?"

By then they were at the door. She thought fleetingly of what she had sacrificed for her mother. Her self-respect, for one thing. There was no real sacrifice involved in entering into a business arrangement, as long as both parties agreed in advance on the rules. For no real reason other than her woman's intuition, she trusted Will Bradford. He was the kind of man who looked you directly in the eye and spoke his mind, like it or not.

One who looked entirely too masculine, entirely too sexy, entirely too attractive...

But that was neither here nor there.

By that time they had reached the judge's office.

Several men were already there. "Sebastian," she greeted, marveling all over again that he would be her baby's half brother. By looking at him now, she might even have a glimpse of the future—of what her own son would look like years from now. Unless he turned out to be a daughter.

Introductions were made, and Diana managed to hang on to her composure by a thread. Having Will's steadying hand under her elbow helped. These were Will's friends. Under other circumstances, if this marriage had been more than a business arrangement, they might have become her friends.

"How do you do?" she murmured calmly, trying to fix each man's face and name in her mind.

Someone made a joke about Will's going to great lengths to keep from picking out a charity. She hadn't the least idea what that was all about and was far too nervous even to wonder. Standing there in her tea-colored silk suit and her only decent pair of heels, she clutched the bouquet Will had handed her when she'd arrived. It had struck her as odd, but a sweet gesture. Fighting panic, she clutched her purse in one hand and the flowers in the other and thought, Business arrangement. Happens every day. Mergers—takeovers.

It wasn't going to be a takeover, not in any sense of the word. She had made that clear from the first. She was doing it to give her baby a name, and Will was doing it because...well, probably because Jack had been his friend, and for all she knew, they could have had an agreement. If anything happened to either of them, the other would look after the survivor's interests.

"Watch it, Danny, you're hyperventilating," Will

whispered as Judge Shirley entered in a swirl of black robes and Georgio perfume.

"No'm not," she whispered back and even managed a stiff-lipped smile. "Don't call me Danny."

For some reason, she recalled stories her mother used to tell her about the early days when a young Lila Smothers had first met the man she had later married. Liam Foster, long-haired, bearded and ponytailed, had played guitar with a group that never quite made it. He'd written poetry that no one who wasn't stoned, drunk or high could appreciate. According to Lila, he had once gone without eating meat products for an entire year protesting cruelty to animals and had been jailed more than once for protesting against the capitalistic establishment.

Funny, the way things had turned out, Diana thought, gripping the stems of her flowers with damp, trembling hands. It was the so-called establishment that had given her mother a job after Liam had wrapped his delivery van around a telephone pole one icy night back in Pennsylvania. It was the establishment that had fought to save her mother's life against insurmountable odds.

And it was the establishment his daughter was marrying into at this very moment.

"Miss Foster?"

"Diana?"

"What?" she snapped, whipping her head around to glare at the man she was about to tie herself to.

"The judge wants to know if you do."

"If I do what?"

Snickering sounded behind her. Someone touched her on the arm. It was Sebastian, who was grinning from ear to ear.

Blinking herself back to the present, Diana said, "Of course I do. That's why we're here, isn't it?"

One of the men—Jason, she thought—chuckled softly. The others tried and failed to control their smiles. Even Will's lips were twitching.

"Well, I do—I said I would, but I still can't imagine why *you* do," she whispered fiercely.

"Matter of fact, neither can I," Will said dryly.

It was all over then but the signing. When documents were placed in front of her, she signed her name, adding Bradford only when Will reminded her. They gathered at the door a few minutes later and Sebastian said, "We've set up a big spread at the club. Judge, you're invited."

"Sorry—traffic court in half an hour. One speeder, two jaywalkers. We're making a killing on crime around these parts."

Evidently, Diana told herself, justice in Royal, Texas, had a sense of humor. Once outside, she braced herself to go celebrate her marriage to a man she hardly knew, in the company of four other men she knew not at all. She might have been involved in more ludicrous situations at some point in her life, but at the moment she couldn't think of a single one.

"Seb, how about driving Diana's car to the club? We'll be right behind you," Will said, taking Diana's keys from her hand and tossing them to Sebastian.

Before Diana could open her mouth to protest, Will took her bouquet and ushered her into a metallic gunmetal-gray luxury sedan. She tried to think of something to say, and decided her silence would probably be more appreciated than any inane remark she could make. Something told her that Will had a low tolerance for small talk.

A low tolerance for women, as well, according to secretarial pool gossip. She remembered the sighs and groans he drew whenever he strode past on his way to purchasing. Her own, included.

"What I wouldn't give to see that man without his shirt on."

"Honey, don't stop there. He can park those boots under my bed any old time."

"Hush, y'all, it's *him!* He just got off the elevator!"

Amazingly enough, she was now Mrs. *Him!*

Did everyone at Wescott Oil know? What did they think—that she'd slept her way to the top?

Well, in a way, she had, only that had never been her intention.

"How do you think Sebastian will do as CEO?" Calmly discussing business on the way to her wedding reception should let him know she wasn't expecting anything more than what he'd offered. His name. Protection for her baby in case anyone should put two and two together and come up with the truth.

He glanced at her as he turned onto Main Street. "He'll do fine."

So much for talking business.

So much for talking anything. If she had her car right now, she'd go home, put on her sweats, jog a fast couple of miles and then get busy going through her mother's things and packing them away. And then she'd tackle Jack's boxes. It was time to sweep out the past in order to make room for the future.

Hugging herself, Diana inhaled a provocative mixture of leather upholstery, wilted wedding bouquet and some subtle masculine cologne that reminded her of tall evergreen trees. Cool, dark and lofty.

Just like the man, she thought, and shivered.

"Did you eat breakfast?"

"Of course." A small portion of whole-grain cereal with two dried apricot halves and a cup of tea. She was eating for two now. No more skipped meals, even if she was feeling queasy—which she had been for the last three mornings in a row.

"I don't know what the menu is, but there'll be champagne and wedding cake."

Great. Just what she needed. "I don't drink much."

"Neither do I, but we can sip a few toasts."

She would sip, but having seen what alcohol—as well as a whole pharmacopoeia of drugs, could do to a body, she would settle for sipping a seltzer with a twist.

Silence prevailed. Will thought, this is a hell of a note. Newlyweds who can't think of a damned thing to say. Maybe he should have paid her off, transferred her to Houston and let it go at that, only his conscience wouldn't have allowed it. The woman was pregnant and Jack probably wouldn't have married her even if he'd still been alive. He'd proved that much by his treatment of Dorian's mother.

Besides, dammit, something about her intrigued him. He might have forgotten how to love, but he hadn't forgotten how to lust. This arrangement would benefit them both. She would have care and protection for her baby, while he would have...

Nothing. Frustration, he thought, reminding himself of the specs he had laid out for their merger.

Gripping the wheel of his late-model luxury sedan, he willed his body into submission. No use in inviting a lot of pointed looks and lewd remarks. The guys were curious enough as it was.

Her car was already parked in the visitor's section when they reached the club. He'd have to see to having it driven to his apartment. Slanting a quick look at her still face as he shut off ignition, Will felt himself growing aroused all over again.

Deep breath. Think of an icy long-neck—think of an icy shower. This is strictly a business arrangement. No more, no less.

She unclipped her seatbelt and shifted a pair of nylon-clad legs, and he added world-class ankles to a growing list of attributes he'd been trying hard to ignore. Things like large, slumberous eyes, a soft, vulnerable mouth, a straight, elegant nose and a long, graceful neck that invited exploration.

She started to let herself out, and he hurried to open her door. It wasn't a militant feminist thing— he'd never seen any signs of that. The best he could figure was that she wasn't used to small courtesies. Jack might have been big on magnanimous gestures, but he'd seldom bothered with gentlemanly manners.

She shivered. The rain that had pounded down for days had ended, bringing down a blast of Alaskan air. The jet stream was really doing a number on them.

Will placed his hand on her back as they walked toward the side entrance. "I'll show you where you can freshen up. Sure you're feeling all right?"

Be a hell of a note if she got sick and everyone guessed she was pregnant. He didn't know how many, if any, of the guys knew about her affair with Jack. If they'd suspected, they'd have kept quiet about it out of consideration for Seb, who had probably guessed, even though he and Jack hadn't been close in years.

The celebration was held in one of the smallest rooms as if to make up for the lack of celebrants. Will had considered asking several other secretaries, but as he wouldn't have known where to draw the line, he'd decided against it. It hadn't occurred to him that she wouldn't have invited a few friends of her own.

He held the door and waited for her to enter. "I'm afraid it turned out to be a stag party. Sorry about that."

"I don't know many people here. We've—that is, I've only been here for a few months, and I've been...busy."

Her mother, he thought. She'd lost her mother shortly after moving to Royal. Hell, she was still grieving for her mother, and he'd pushed her into a marriage she didn't want. Talk about timing!

Her lips were trembling. Acting purely on impulse, he leaned over and kissed her. "Bear up, Mrs. Bradford. Half an hour or so and we can go home, kick off our shoes and turn on T.V. You like old movies?"

Blinking back tears after the fleeting kiss, Diana collected her wits enough to say, "Actually, I do. Is that your idea of a proper celebration?" And then she turned beet red. "I didn't— What I meant was—"

"Hush, honey, I know what you meant. Look, we'll just play it by ear, shall we? We got along just fine clearing out Jack's office. No reason why we can't go on the same way."

Dammit, he hadn't meant to drag Jack's name into

it. She needed to put the past behind her so that they could forge some kind of a workable relationship.

A champagne cork popped. Someone had brought in a few balloons, strung a few streamers. Will thought it looked absurd in the masculine realm of the Texas Cattleman's Club, but he supposed he appreciated the gesture.

"I think they're waiting on you to cut the cake." He indicated the five-tier confection gracing the center of the round table. "You want to try a few of the nibbles first?"

She nodded, looking warily at the dark paneled walls festooned with white ribbons and foil-covered bells draped over the heavy frames of paintings of several famous and obviously well-endowed bulls.

Will glared at Sebastian, wondering if he'd done it deliberately. It was more in line with Jason's puckish sense of humor, but it might have been a joint effort.

Or purely unintentional.

Dammit, he didn't need any reminders. This was his wedding day, only there wasn't going to be a wedding night. At least, not in the traditional sense. But, of course, the guys couldn't have known that.

"Are they all waiting for me to go first?" she whispered.

"I think so. Otherwise, they'd be pigging out. These guys aren't known for their reserve." Wasn't *that* the truth!

He took a thin, gold-banded plate and loaded it with finger food. Diana eyed it warily. Her queasiness wasn't restricted to mornings. The buffalo wings she'd pass on. The cheese and salsa on rye crackers was a possibility. The black bean dip looked good, so she helped herself to a spoonful and took half a dozen more crackers.

"So, tell me, Di, what did you see in this guy? Did he tell you he was a hotshot cowboy? Bet he forgot to tell you his own horse threw him once and he was laid up for three weeks." That was from Jason. She was getting to know them a bit better.

"The horse was spooked by a rattlesnake while I was trying to talk on my cell phone, or it never would have happened," Will grumbled.

"Somehow, being an Easterner, I never pictured cowboys riding the range while they talked on cell phones." Diana found herself relaxing enough to share the joke. "Some states have a law about using the phone while you're driving."

And so it went—teasing, tall tales. At first the laughter was stiff, but soon it became more relaxed. They were all obviously trying to make her feel welcome, but she suspected they were curious as to why their friend would marry with no warning at all. Especially a woman he'd never even dated. What did they think the two of them had been doing up on the eleventh floor all those days when they'd worked together to clear out Jack's things?

"Cake time!" Sebastian announced. Diana was still a bit hazy on the others, but everyone at Wescott Oil knew Sebastian, the heir to his father's empire.

It was Keith—she thought—who said, "Let me move it closer so you can reach it."

White frosting, pure sugar. White cake, pure refined carbohydrate. In just the short time since she'd learned she was pregnant she'd become far more health conscious, but this was no time to be picky.

"Hold your plates," she said, and grimly attacked the fancy confection.

There was some teasing after that about whose cake they'd be cutting next. Something about a bet, which she'd heard referred to before. Will edged closer. "You're not eating. Nerves?"

"Oh, no…it's…it looks delicious!"

"Diana? You want to level with me?" asked Will. "If you're dieting, then don't. You could carry ten more pounds, easy, and still look like a million bucks."

So she nibbled a cracker dipped in black beans and salsa, praying she wouldn't get sick. He was standing close enough so that she could see the gold shards in his hazel eyes. Warily she said, "It's not that—I mean, thank you. I think. But I don't eat sweets very much."

"Not even your own wedding cake?" With his own fork he cut a bite of her cake and held it to her lips. "Come on, sweetheart—open up."

She let the endearment pass. He was obviously doing it for his friends' benefit, and she appreciated it, she really did. Leaning forward, she bit off what he was offering. This was her wedding day, after all. She could afford to make a few allowances.

Two of the men were discussing inducting someone or other into the club. Did grown men do that kind of thing? she wondered.

Later she asked Will about it, and without telling her who the honoree was to be, he admitted that, yeah, they did. "Frankly it strikes me as pretty juvenile, but tradition rules in an outfit like this. He'll be asked to address the membership committee at a black-tie dinner on the ten most embarrassing moments of his life and the ten things of which he's the proudest. That pretty well sizes a man up, don't you think?''

Come to think about it, she agreed it did. She wished she dared to ask those same questions of her new husband.

The others had champagne. Will arranged for her to be served a sparkling cider. She wrinkled her nose, half expecting the bubbles to tickle. She'd read that in so many books—the bubbles always tickled the heroine's nose. In her case they didn't, but since she was pretending to be the heroine of this farce—not a princess, but close enough—she might as well play the part properly.

''Ready to go home and kick back with a good video?''

''You read my mind. Actually, I wouldn't mind getting out of these shoes,'' she whispered.

He grinned, and she told herself that if he had truly read her mind, he'd know just how terrified she was of losing control of her life again. After growing up as she had in an abusive situation, she had vowed never to hand over control of her life to anyone. It had been her choice not to try for a college scholarship, but to take the secretarial course instead. Secretaries were always in demand, as she'd told her mother. It was a highly portable skill.

It had been her choice to move all the way across the country when her mother had apparently lost all interest in everything, including her job. That was when Diana had learned that no one has complete control over their life. Shortly after they'd settled in, she'd had another choice to make. Whether or not to trade an affair with a man nearly twice her age for her mother's health care. She hadn't been at Wescott Oil long enough for her company insurance to kick in, and even then, preexisting conditions would have been excluded.

She had made the decision.

And now she had made another decision. To marry a stranger in order to legalize and protect her baby. That meant she was still in control...didn't it?

"You can drop me off at my apartment," she said a few minutes after they left in a flurry of best wishes and ribald remarks. She told him the address. "I can always walk to work and pick up my car on the way home tomorrow. One of the things I like about living in a small town—almost everything's within walking distance."

In some of the neighborhoods where she'd lived with her mother over the past few years, she had quickly learned that walking was not an option. Shortly after that they would pull up stakes and move again, hoping for something better. Always hoping...

"Depends on what you call a 'walking distance.'" Idling at the stoplight, Will turned to study her averted face.

"Three miles a day, at least five days a week?"

He shot her an admiring look. "Nice going. But another thing about small towns—it's hard to keep secrets."

Her stricken look made him wish he'd kept his mouth shut.

"What I meant was that there was some speculation about you and Jack. A gated community like Pine Valley is hardly the best place to carry on a clandestine affair."

"I hate that word."

"Affair?"

"Clandestine. As if we'd been sneaking around like a couple of underage kids. Anyway, mostly we stayed at his cabin."

He drove past her turnoff, and she sat up, alarmed. "I live on Macauley Street. The Lennox Apartments." It was an old building, hanging on to respectability by a thread, but it was all she'd been able to afford at the time they'd moved to Royal.

"Like I said, small towns are big on gossip," he said. "We both know the reason for this marriage. It's hardly a love match." Damn. Why not rub it in? Will mocked himself silently.

Not by so much as a flicker of an eyelash did her expression change, but her mouth—too large, too naked, too vulnerable—seemed to tighten just a bit. "Don't you ever wear makeup?" he asked, irritated for no good reason.

"I always wear makeup." It was a lie and they both knew it. Her kind of skin didn't require any enhancement. "I must have chewed off my lipstick. Sometimes I do that when I'm nervous. There's no room in this purse to carry much makeup." She held up something that was roughly the size and shape of a business envelope. "My other one's a black leather tote—hardly suitable for wedding wear."

He pulled into the parking area behind his own apartment complex. It wasn't up to Pine Valley standards, but it served his purpose. He'd never been big on status symbols. Switching off the engine, he stared through a row of carefully nurtured Leyland cypresses at the sunset—like an abstract painting done in shades of gray, gold and copper.

Now what? He asked himself. Some genius had

once said, "Begin as you mean to go on," or words to that effect. In their case it meant giving her a key, not carrying her over the threshold.

His palms were damp. Any kind of marriage, no matter what the reasons behind it, was a big step for a guy who'd avoided entanglements as long as he had. Even with all the safeguards, no man with half a grain of sense went into something like this without a few reservations.

She didn't wear perfume—at least, not the kind that announced her presence the minute she entered a room. Yet, oddly enough, he was more aware of her than he'd been of any woman in a long, long time. The subtle scent of her skin—her soap and shampoo...

"I think we pretty well understand each other," he said with a calmness that hid an increasing number of doubts. He would like to attribute the edginess he was feeling to filling up with junk food in the middle of the afternoon. "I should have scheduled things so that we could at least have a decent meal afterward. I didn't plan the party, that was Seb's idea."

"It was a lovely idea. I like your friends. They don't seem to—I mean, well—the fact that I was Sebastian's father's secretary..."

As well as his mistress. The words hung in the cool air, unspoken.

Diana unclipped her seat belt but made no move to get out. "Don't they think it's odd that we got married the way we did?"

"You mean in the courthouse instead of the church?"

"I mean you being who you are and me being who I am. We hardly even know each other."

"Who we are is irrelevant. As for the rest—why we married, that's nobody's business but ours."

What could he say? That they'd taken one look at each other and fallen madly in love? The guys would never buy it, not in a million years. After his first brief marriage, Will had made a point of avoiding long-term relationships.

Besides which, Seb probably knew about her relationship with Jack. As for the others, he couldn't say. For a bunch of guys who had shared more than a few high-risk escapades, they respected each other's privacy. Maybe he could remind them of an article he'd read recently about the increased life span of married men.

He went around to open her door. She sat there, making no move to get out. "Uh, Mrs. Bradford, we're home."

"*You're* home. I told you where I live."

"Look, Diana, one of the reasons we both agreed to this deal was to obscure the fact that in a few months you're going to be having Jack's baby. Another little Wescott contender. Or have you changed your mind about keeping it?"

"No," she whispered.

"Right. Then we stick together for the duration. As a cover, I'll admit it's pretty thin, but it won't even stand a chance if we live apart." She sat there while he held the door open. The insulation on a few more overworked nerves began to unravel. "You don't want to move in with me? Fine, we'll stay at your place. Just let me run in and grab a few things for tonight. I can move the rest later."

Diana looked up in horror at the thought of having him see where she lived. The thrift-shop specials, the things her mother had dragged all the way across the country. Tacky remnants of an idealistic age that had largely ended before she'd even been born.

"No—that is, we might as well stay here, but I'll need something to sleep in. Some personal items."

"I can lend you something to sleep in tonight, and I probably have a spare toothbrush, but if you'd rather, we can go back now and pack whatever you'll need for the next few days. It's early yet."

She was tempted.

Actually she was tempted to crawl into bed, pull the covers over her head and pretend none of this had ever happened. Pretend her mother was still alive, listening to Joan Baez on the stereo while she wove her beaded macramé wall hangings. Or playing along on her old Gibson guitar that wouldn't stay tuned because the tuning gears were shot.

Pretend she herself wasn't pregnant, much less married to a man who both attracted and repelled her because he was too large, too reserved and too domineering, if only in the nicest possible way.

"Well…tomorrow, I guess. I can go by after breakfast. Do you have a kitchen in your apartment?"

He grinned, his lean cheeks that were already showing signs of what used to be called five-o'clock shadow before it became fashionable, creasing in a pair of unlikely dimples. "I thought you'd never ask."

Four

This had to be the strangest wedding night in recorded history, Diana told herself a few hours later as she sat cross-legged on a large leather covered couch, eating curried garbanzos and watching a video of an old World War II submarine movie.

She slanted a look at her bridegroom, sprawled in a massive lounger, his eyes half-closed. His five-o'clock shadow was now a fledgling beard. He was barefoot, wearing jeans and what must once have been a black T-shirt. Thanks to improper laundering, it was now a mottled shade of purple. Quite a change from the well-dressed executive whose department took up the entire tenth floor of the eleven-story Wescott Building.

Absently, Will held out a bowl of popcorn, and she helped herself to a handful. He'd offered to grill steaks, but she'd been feeling queasy again. So much for morning sickness. In her case, it was an equal-opportunity affliction.

"I've been wondering—where am I supposed to report for work on Monday?" She waited for a lull in the dialogue to ask, but the question had been bothering her. She no longer had an office.

Did she even have a job?

"I wouldn't be in any great rush to go back to work. Take a few days off. It's expected of honeymooners."

She sent him a mocking look. "Oh? And how long are you going to take off?"

"About a week should do it. I thought we might drive out to the ranch for a few days. You like horses?"

Horses? He expected her to go horseback riding? In her condition? Was it safe, even if she knew how? "Well, I don't exactly dislike them. Actually, I've never met one."

"I'll introduce you. We'll start out nice and easy and let nature take its course."

Was he talking about her and his horse or her and their business-arrangement marriage?

On the TV screen, terror stalked in the form of a pair of swift, silent torpedoes. In black-and-white, on a small screen, the horror was no less potent. While Will sat seemingly relaxed and watched, Diana studied him. Studied his hands, which lay relaxed on his thighs. Studied the length—not to mention the strength—of his long legs.

Oh, she'd noticed him, all right, on the few occasions their paths had crossed at work. What woman wouldn't? Even if his looks had been ordinary, the way he carried himself—assured without being noticeably arrogant, would have earned him more than a few admiring glances. At close range he radiated a tightly leashed sexuality that Jack, for all his polish, all his wealth and efforts, had never managed to achieve.

Jack had mentioned once that Will never used the private gym he had set up for senior employees. Could horseback riding have developed those long, smooth muscles?

He caught her studying his rugged profile, and she hurriedly lowered her eyes. "It's nice. Your apartment. Have you lived here long?"

Oh, for Pete's sake! *Hello, cowboy, where're you from?*

Her mother would have asked him his sign by now, and told him more than he ever wanted to know about his traits, his future and his love life. Astrology had rated right up there with folk music and beaded macramé among her mother's early passions.

"About ten years. It's comfortable," he said in answer to the questions she'd forgotten she'd asked.

For a man rumored to be extremely wealthy, it had come as something of a surprise, Will's apartment. It was spacious, but hardly luxurious. The floors were carpeted in a muted neutral, the walls a slightly deeper shade of the same color. Fawn, perhaps. There were no pictures on the wall, not even any family photographs. The furniture, oak and leather, for the most part, was probably hideously expensive, but it had been chosen for comfort rather than style. Books overflowed the bookshelves and were stacked on the floor, along with videos.

The guest bedroom was small, but more than adequate.

"You mentioned a spare toothbrush?" She forced a yawn and followed it with a genuine one. And then another. "Mercy, it's been a long day."

"You feeling all right? You're not, uh—feeling upset or anything, are you?"

"No, I'm fine." And she would be, once her hormones settled down and she got back on a regular schedule. "As long as I remember to eat and don't get stressed out, I'm in great health. The morning sickness is only temporary. It shouldn't last much longer."

He eyed her intently, making her wonder why hazel eyes were so underrated. *Piercing* was the word that came to mind.

Smoldering was the word that followed. Like banked coals.

"Wake me anytime if you need anything, promise? Anything at all. I'm a light sleeper."

Suddenly she was fighting tears. When had *anyone* ever made that offer? Her mother hadn't, not in a long, long time. It would never have occurred to Jack. He'd paid her mother's hospitalization, which had been more than generous of him, but he had never wanted to hear about Diana's personal needs, her fears, her hopes.

It had never occurred to her to share them with him.

"Thanks," she said gruffly. "I'm an early riser, but I'll try to be quiet."

"No problem." He stood, unfolding his six-foot-plus length from the dark-brown recliner. "Coffee, tea or decaf?"

"For breakfast? Coffee if you have it. The real

thing. I'll have to taper off caffeine soon, but I'd rather do it gradually.''

Will lay awake, his mind taking off down a few strange pathways. He was married again. Something he could have sworn he would never be. The first time had hurt too damned much, for too damned long.

Somewhere along the line, his brief marriage nearly twenty years earlier to Shelly of the infectious laughter, the flashing blue eyes, the sexy sulks that always ended in bed, had faded like an old photograph exposed to the light too long. When had that happened? He'd been too busy to notice, but obviously today's events had stirred a few ashes.

They were nothing at all alike, his two wives.

But then, he was nothing like the eager young gy-rene he'd been when he'd married, fresh out of boot camp. He'd owned the world then—a gorgeous bride and a promising career as a marine.

It had all come crashing down the day some drugged-up, two-bit hood had broken into their du-plex. He'd headed straight for the bedroom and Shelly's jewelry case. Hearing something, she'd come up from the basement where she'd been doing the laundry, and he had shoved her back down the stairs.

At least she hadn't suffered. According to the au-thorities, she had died instantly of a broken neck. Someone in the neighborhood had seen the punk run-ning across the backyard to the woods beyond and reported it. He'd been picked up, tried for man-slaughter and sentenced to ten years, which in Will's estimation was a joke. An insult. A slap on the wrist.

Will had been sent back to the States. Vowing to be waiting for the murdering son of a gun the day he got out of prison, he had grimly served out the rest of his hitch. By the time he left the service, his lust for revenge had faded just enough for common sense to take over.

Instead of setting himself up for a murder charge, he'd moved across the country. Still driven by anger and grief, he had earned a degree in accounting. Numbers were emotionless, exact—both qualities that had appealed to him back then.

Eventually the raw wound had healed over, but the scars were a permanent part of him. Over the years he had managed to fill a few of the hollow places inside him with challenging work, new friends and a few sub rosa missions with other members of the Cattleman's Club. Not to mention half a dozen charities he funded anonymously. What more could a man expect out of life?

Sex, came the instant answer.

But *not* with his wife.

It was going to be a long, dry spell. He had taken certain vows. Not in a church, but nonetheless binding. For the next year or two, until Diana and the child were ready to move on with their own lives, he would abide by those promises.

It was still dark the next morning when Will rolled over, groaned and sat up in his rumpled bed. Too many champagne toasts hadn't done his head any good. While it was still dark, he might run a few miles to clear away the static. This time of morning the sidewalks would be empty.

In honor of having a woman under his roof, he'd

slept in sweats instead of his usual nothing. They would do to run in, as he was no more inclined to wear suitable running gear than he was to drive out to the park and jog along a designated track. His method of waking up his body was more efficient. Get up, get it done, get to work.

On the ranch, unloading a truckload of hay, checking a few miles of fence and maybe going after the big cat that had been spooking his mares would have done it.

In town he was forced to improvise.

She was in his kitchen. "Hi," she said, her soft voice husky with sleep. "Hope you don't mind, but I warned you, I'm an early riser."

"No. I mean, that's great—uh, I don't suppose you'd like to go for a short run with me?"

Glancing down at the oversize gray sweats he'd lent her to sleep in and her bare feet, she said, "Hardly. I'd better go home and pack a few things."

"Yeah, sure." Her skin had a pink glow that he knew damned well didn't come from cosmetics. She'd braided her hair, but it was half-unraveled. There was something different about her—a certain softness instead of her usual patrician aloofness.

Yeah, softness—that was it. He'd lay odds that softness was hardly a quality the cool, conservatively dressed Miss Foster aspired to.

Amused for no real reason, he said, "Good morning, Mrs. Bradford," and damned if she didn't blush. Hell, he was only teasing—he hadn't meant anything by it. At least, nothing personal.

"My car—you said you were going to have it driven to my apartment?"

"Right. Look, I don't feel like running, anyway.

My head would probably fall off and roll down a storm drain before I reached the end of the block. How about we have some coffee, think about breakfast, then I'll drive you to your place and you can take your time packing and drive your car back here when you're finished.''

While she was considering the offer, the coffeemaker gurgled its last gasp. Reaching past her for a mug, Will was conscious of the heat of her body and the scent of soap and toothpaste and woman.

How personal could you get? Good thing his sweats were baggy.

"Okay, coffee. I've already nibbled some saltines—I think things are settling down by now."

He offered to cook bacon and eggs, and she said politely, "Thank you. One slice, one egg, both well done, please."

"Hey, you're eating for two now, don't forget."

"I'm also about to outgrow everything I own, so let's not rush the process."

She smiled. He chuckled. Some of the tension faded, but as his kitchen was small, physical contact was a given. Her arm brushed his shoulder when she reached for plates. He backed into her as he opened the massive stainless-steel refrigerator, muttered an apology and then stepped on her toe.

"Well, hell," he said plaintively. "It's not like I ever won any waltzing contests, but normally I'm slightly less clumsy than a three-legged ox."

It wasn't as if they hadn't worked in close confines before, either. While Jack's office was certainly spacious, there was only so much room in front of a filing cabinet. He must have managed to bump into her a dozen times—looking back, it might even have been deliberate. But that had been different.

Yeah, she wasn't your wife then.

"Crazy weather we're having, huh?" Go ahead, Bradford, impress her with your brilliant conversation.

"Did you mean what you said last night?"

He rifled through his brain, searching for any indiscretion he might have committed. "Uh, you mean about...?"

"Going to your ranch?"

He let out his breath in a sigh of relief, poured two mugs of coffee and flipped the bacon. One slice for her, two for him, when he could easily have put away half a dozen. Jack's death had been a warning. "Sure, if you'd like to go. Matter of fact, I've been thinking about taking a month off, maybe spending a couple of weeks at the ranch and then heading for salt water to do some serious fishing. You like fishing?"

She was beating up the eggs while he cooked the bacon. She added a dash of salt, a dash of black pepper, and he started to suggest a whopping dollop of *salsa con queso*—the hot variety—but decided the baby might not care for it.

"Fishing? I don't know, I've never tried it." She handed him the bowl and he poured the eggs in the pan and stirred while she made toast. Nothing like teamwork.

"You like seafood?" he asked. Breakfast with a woman was a new experience. He hadn't had time to get used to it when he was married the first time, and since then, his dalliances had rarely included breakfast.

"Hmm," she said, and bit her lip. He watched, wondering what it felt like. Soft. Moist. Naked…vulnerable. Maybe there was a reason why women wore lipstick. In men, war paint was used to lend a feeling of invincibility.

Not until they had sampled the fare did she speak again. "If by seafood you mean frozen breaded fish sticks, then not particularly. Canned tuna is okay—I've never tried clams, but I looked at a raw oyster once, and it was horribly icky. I could never eat one."

Will tilted back his chair and laughed until his headache reminded him that he needed to take a couple of aspirin tablets. "We'll break you in easy, shall we? I'll take you to Claire's for some mountain trout. Did Jack take you there?"

The question lay between them like a dead horse.

"Actually, Jack never took me anywhere. We were—that is, we tried…"

"I know, I know. Look, I'm sorry. Like I said, I never won any waltzing contests, and waltzing around the obvious comes under that heading." Might as well lay it all out on the table, between the apple jelly and the Texas Pete. "For what it's worth, Diana, I doubt if too many people knew about you and Jack, so why don't we start today with us. You and me. Not you and Jack and me."

"How about you and me and Jack's baby?" She blotted her lips on a paper napkin, which was the only kind he had.

"How about you and me and *your* baby? By the time it's born it'll be our baby."

Suddenly her eyes were flooded with tears. She laughed, a soft, broken sound that twisted his gut.

"Sorry—I'm not crying, honestly I'm not. It's these hormones of mine. At least it's better than having to rush to the bathroom to be sick every morning."

"I never knew about any of this stuff. About pregnancy, I mean. And listen, Diana, before you go getting the wind up about what I said—I mean, about it being our baby—no way would I ever try to take him away from you. For any reason. I just want to do what I think Jack would have done—that is, to look after you until you're on your feet again."

Liar, he thought. Jack would've bought her a one-way ticket out of town.

She yawned, and he said, "Why don't we leave the dishes and go for a walk. Not a run—you probably shouldn't be running, anyway, in case you—uh, jar something loose."

"Honestly, I'm not always like this," she said, laughing, then yawning again.

"Hey, I understand. Besides, even Sleeping Beauty eventually woke up, didn't she?"

Rising, Will set his dishes on the counter, then impulsively leaned down and kissed her. There was nothing at all sexual about it, and she told herself that what she was feeling—the simmering warmth, the neediness—was only hormones.

Well, of course it is, you ninny! she thought. What do you think drives a woman's libido?

That afternoon she called the clinic and asked to speak to Dr. Woodbury.

"He's out, but if I can help you? I'm Kelly Cartwright, the nurse practitioner."

"Oh. Well, my name is Diana Foster, uh, Bradford. I was in a few weeks ago, and…well, I'm pregnant, and—"

"Just let me pull your chart, Ms. Foster-Bradford."

"It would be under Foster, but call me Diana...please."

"Okay, Diana, you were suffering the usual symptoms, morning sickness, sleepiness, right?"

"The morning sickness seems to have stopped, but now I can't seem to stay awake. Besides that, I cry at nothing at all. Last night I started crying in the middle of an old Smothers Brothers video. Is this normal? I mean, I don't even show yet. What's going to happen once I get really going on this thing?"

The nurse practitioner, who invited Diana to call her Kelly, laughed. "The only thing you have to watch is your nibbling. Stick to pickles and low-fat ice cream, and you'll be just fine. Luckily, you can afford to gain at least twenty pounds, but let's not do it all at once, shall we? As for other symptoms, you might even skip the heartburn, but chances are, you'll be sticking pretty close to a bathroom as more pressure is put on your bladder. Oh, and sex is just fine until you get close to term. We'll talk about it when you come in."

Sex was just fine? Well, great. Now that she was married to a man who could curl her toes with a single sweep of his eyelashes, sex was not an option.

Talk about life's little ironies.

After making an appointment, she settled back in Will's marvelously comfortable chair. She had a feeling it wasn't one of those that could be had in any furniture store. It was brown cowhide, with creases and natural scars showing. Her mother would have hated it. She'd have wanted to cover it with a zebra-print throw.

Oh, Mama, I wish you could be here. I need to talk to you. We always had each other, but now I don't have anyone at all.

For a long time she sat and thought about the crazy route her life had taken. From Shinglehouse, Pennsylvania, to Royal, Texas, with half a dozen stops along the way. There was no knowing how long her mother had been ill, as the symptoms didn't manifest until nearly the end. The daughter of a New England clergyman who had disowned her after she'd run away to something called a love-in, Lila Smithers Foster had made her share of mistakes, but in her own way she'd been a good mother. She would have made a wonderful grandmother, Diana thought tearfully.

She dried her eyes, then thought about the way Will had accepted her mother's idea of decorating as graciously as if Martha Stewart had done the job. She'd tried her best to keep him from helping her move, but he was too much the gentleman.

"Honey, we can't have you straining yourself," he'd said. "You do the packing, I'll do the donkey work."

So she'd unlocked the door, painfully conscious of the posters, the lumpy, uneven, hemp wall hangings, the tacky lava lamp and the leopard-print throw on the back of the thrift-shop sofa. For someone who hated the use of animal products, her mother had dearly loved animal prints. Then there were the dried flowers in lumpy, unglazed pots thrown by long-forgotten potters. And her mother's old Gibson propped in a corner in the battered hardshell case decorated with peace symbols and painted daisies.

Will had carried it out to the car as carefully as if it had been a Stradivarius.

Diana had stared at the stack of tattered music that neither she nor her mother could read, and teared up again. Her mother had taught her the words and they'd sung together, old songs from the days of protests and idealism. Songs filled with hope, which—at least in her mother's case—had died a long and painful death.

"It's going to take a while," she'd warned her new husband, looking at all the boxes she'd packed and left stacked in her mother's bedroom.

"No hurry. Pack what you'll need and I'll have someone come in and do the rest."

"I'd rather do it myself. I know it's not much, but my mother was— That is, she was—"

"Your mother," he'd said quietly.

She'd had to swallow hard several times to keep from bawling her eyes out all over again. The man was almost *too* kind.

She'd left the furnishings—after all, the lease still had almost a month to go—but she'd taken a few things, such as the guitar and a matted watercolor some long-ago unknown artist had done that she particularly liked.

Somewhat to her surprise, Will had liked it, too. He'd insisted on having it framed for her. He brought it back from the framers on the way home the next day, and now he wanted to hang it in the living room.

Predictably Diana burst into tears. "You shouldn't," she sobbed.

"We can hang it in the guest room if you don't want it in here. It needs to be kept under glass for protection against air pollution, though. The framer said it probably wouldn't have lasted much longer unframed.''

When had his arms closed around her? When had she wrapped her own arms around his neck?

She cried some more, then hiccuped a few times, and then she laughed. ''Is there a medal for men who take on the care and feeding of newly pregnant women? I think I must have saved up a lifetime of tears just waiting for a handy shoulder to drench.''

He laughed, and then he kissed her, salty tears and all. She thought, if only she hadn't messed up her life so thoroughly. If only she could have had waited....

''Yeah, I know, it's the hormones,'' he murmured. ''I should have guessed right off when you tackled me with that triple cone of chocolate.'' She had told him what the nurse practitioner had said about the quirky symptoms of early pregnancy. ''Besides which,'' he added gently, ''I suspect you're hauling around a lot of baggage you need to get out of your system.''

If only he knew. ''You're never going to let me live that down, are you?'' She pulled away, her lips still tingling from a kiss that had been over almost as quickly as it had begun. Soft, almost tentative, there'd been nothing at all sexual about it.

Correction. Everything about this man was sexual, only he hadn't intended it that way, and she had no business interpreting it that way.

Hugging herself, Diana watched as he hammered a nail into his pristine wall and hung the newly framed watercolor. She pictured his long, lean, muscular body wearing nothing at all instead of the body-

hugging chambray shirt and blue jeans he wore to
relax in.

Among the symptoms the nurse had mentioned
was a heightened libido. Which had to explain, Diana
rationalized, why she found herself picturing him in
her bed, in her arms, sharing her afternoon naps and
making slow, sweet love to her. Whispering words
that no man had ever said to her—words about love
and together and forever....

Five

Will poured himself a cup of coffee, the morning paper tucked under his arm, and then settled down to read the business section. He needed to go by the office this morning. He would leave a note for Diana, suggesting that when she felt like it, she might drive over to her old place, pack a few more things, and he would pick them up this afternoon. The more of her belongings she surrounded herself with, the sooner she would adapt.

Or so he told himself. Pregnant women were a breed apart, he was discovering.

The market was taking another nosedive. Tech stocks down heavily—utilities holding. Thank God. Will scanned the section, then went back and glanced at headlines—no surprises there. He was on the sports section when he heard the bathroom door close.

By the time he'd finished his coffee and dressed in modified business attire—casual suit, no tie—he heard the shower cut off. Might as well wait instead of leaving a note. They were honeymooning, after all. It wouldn't do to rush downtown too early.

A few minutes later she emerged, flush-faced, in a cloud of talcum-scented steam, wearing a yellow flannel bathrobe, her hair covered by a towel.

"Oh! You startled me. You're already dressed. Are we going somewhere?"

"I've been thinking—why don't we close out the lease on the Lennox place and move all your things here. We can rent a storage unit for whatever we can't fit in."

"You're kidding...right?"

"Why would I do that?"

"Will, look at this place." She waved her arms expressively, so he looked. It was your typical upper-end apartment. Nothing outstanding. Certainly not as...distinctive, he thought for want of a better term, as her own apartment. Having noticed her when she'd first come to work at Wescott Oil, he could vouch for Diana's taste. While not expensive, it was impeccable—which meant someone else was responsible for the decor of her old apartment. Chances were, it had been her mother.

"Thanks for letting me bring as much as I did, but most of what's left came from the local thrift shop. It can go back there once I'm finished with it."

"You're finished with it." Will knew the moment the words left his tongue it was the wrong thing to say. "That is, you can take your time. Naturally, you'll stay here, though."

She grabbed the towel with both hands, gave her

hair a thorough rubbing, then looked him squarely in the eye. "Don't tell me what to do. Please. I make my own decisions."

He swore softly. "Don't yank my chain, lady. I've got troubles enough at work without adding any domestic games."

She took a deep breath that caused her robe to gape open, revealing the soft swell of her breasts. "Let me put it another way. There's nothing domestic involved here. Ours is strictly a business arrangement. We both agreed to that, else I'd never have gone through with it. And I certainly I don't remember anything in our agreement that says you get to take control of my life now."

"You're ready to give up on this so soon? Come on, Danny, girl—give me another chance." His tone was openly mocking, his deep-set eyes glinting with something that might—or might not—be amusement.

Wariness came over her like a dark shadow. She wrapped her robe more closely around her body. "Yes, well...I just wanted to be sure we understood each other."

He said nothing, his very silence an invitation to babble on, to try desperately to explain something she didn't understand herself. "I mean, it's not as if we were— Well, you know..."

"No I don't. We aren't what, Danny?"

"We aren't really married!"

"We're not? Funny—I distinctly remember paying for a license. The judge said all the right words. At least I don't think she left out anything important. We both signed certain documents. In my book, that makes us legally wed." He knew what she was trying to say, but he wasn't ready to let her off the hook.

If there was one thing he insisted on in both his business and his personal dealings—and marriage was the most personal of all—it was honesty. Square dealing.

She flung out her arms again. Funny, he'd never noticed the way she used gestures to emphasize her words. "Haven't you ever heard of a marriage of convenience, for mercy's sake? Read a romance! Half of them are based on marriages of convenience!"

"Why?"

"Why what?" She blinked. Freshly scrubbed, free of any possible enhancement, lashes like hers should be registered as lethal weapons.

"Why are marriages of convenience considered romantic?"

She took a deep breath, crossed her arms over her modest bosom, and he thought, Aha! Gotcha!

"How do I know? I'm no expert on romance. Look, can we please change the subject? You're all dressed to go out somewhere, and I've got loads of things I need to do today."

Name one, he wanted to say, but didn't. His gaze moved over her, this woman he had married because it had seemed like the honorable thing to do and he was in a position to do it. And, yeah, because she intrigued him. "I'm going in to work for a few hours. I'm not telling you where to go or what to do, but I'd appreciate not having to track you down. Might spoil the illusion we're trying to create." He didn't bother to hide the sarcasm.

Funny thing—he seldom resorted to sarcasm. The lady had a talent for bringing out hidden facets of his personality.

"All right," she said grudgingly. "But anytime you change your mind and want to get out of this marriage, it's just fine with me. I didn't suggest it in the first place, if you'll remember. If you're afraid Sebastian might be embarrassed about the baby, then I can leave town. In fact, I'd planned to relocate." Her rich-brown eyes took on a militant sparkle. "But just so you know, I don't need you or anyone else to take care of me. I've been taking care of myself all my adult life—even before that."

Will wasn't in the habit of badgering anyone, especially not a woman. Especially not a woman he was married to—and especially not about matters such as the one they were discussing now.

Taking a deep, steadying breath, he scratched his jaw and apologized. "I guess I came on too strong." He wasn't about to admit that, convenient or not, she and her baby were now his responsibility. He was learning what set her off and what he could get away with.

"I guess you did. But you need to understand that being in control of my own life is important to me. I, um, I might have overreacted, too." If her quick, tremulous smile was meant to disarm, it did the trick. "And we haven't really known each other very long."

"Or very well. I think it's about time to change that, don't you?"

She came away from the wall as if she'd backed into a live wire. "Oh, well, as to that, I think we're doing just fine. I mean, look at the way we work together in the kitchen. And I'm even learning to like old submarine movies."

Slowly he shook his head. "Diana, Diana. What

am I going to do with you?'' He knew what he'd like to do, but it wasn't going to happen. That hadn't been a part of the bargain. ''What do you say we head out of town and take it easy for a few days after I get done at the office? You might want to check with your friend at the clinic about riding. Horses, that is.''

His grin had been purely wicked, Diana thought a few hours later as she dressed for her first visit to a real working ranch. She thought they might have clarified their relationship, but she couldn't be sure. Just when she thought she understood where he was coming from, he moved.

Her mother used to say, ''Just when I think I know where it's at, it moves.''

Evidently knowing ''where it was at'' was big back in the seventies.

Diana didn't even know what *it* was, much less where.

She must have yawned a dozen times between looking over the old apartment to see if there was anything she needed to bring back with her and dragging out her suitcase to pack for a weekend on a real ranch.

A ranch! Imagine that. After all her childish fantasies, she was going to get to play cowgirl.

With a real live cowboy, too. Better watch it, princess.

She yawned some more over sandwiches eaten at the bar in the kitchen after Will returned from the office. ''Honestly, it's not the company, it's one of the early symptoms of pregnancy,'' she said after apologizing. "I wonder if anyone ever slept through the entire nine months."

Will was watching the noon business report and only murmured, "Hmm."

Greenspan said something about creeping inflation, and Diana reminded herself to go easy on the mayo from now on. Her waistbands were already getting a bit snug. On the other hand, it had been almost two days since she'd felt the slightest queasiness.

"What were you saying?" he asked when a commercial came on.

"I was saying that I can stay awake now for hours without yawning."

"The question is, can you stay on a horse without falling off?"

"Was Roy Rogers's horse named Trigger?"

"That good, huh?"

"You're not the only one who likes old movies. I used to watch cowboy movies every Saturday morning. Why do you think I moved to Texas?"

"Let me guess. The lush jungles? The ice-capped mountains?"

The gentle teasing was still new enough to cause flutters in her modest bosom. The bosom that would probably grow a full cup size, if the pamphlets she'd read could be believed.

Would he notice?

Do you want him to notice?

As unlikely as it was that she could ever have become the mistress of a wealthy oil tycoon, Diana marveled even more at finding herself married to a man like William K. Bradford, who'd been referred

to by several women in the secretarial pool as a
hunky stud.

Or maybe it was a studly hunk. Either description
applied, although, according to rumor he never
mixed business with pleasure.

She was beginning to wonder about that. He was
still wearing his business suit, and they were both
taking pleasure in the sandwiches she'd created from
practically nothing. Cheese, salsa and bacon on pum-
pernickel.

"What does the *K* stand for?" she asked a couple
of hours later as they left the outskirts of Royal behind and headed southwest. She had packed her
black slacks, two pairs of jeans, two pullover sweat-
ers and her warmest fleece jacket.

Will downshifted for a patch of sand that had
blown across the highway. "King," he said grimly.
"No cracks, please."

"I wouldn't think of it," she murmured with mock
solemnity. And then, in the same solemn tone,
"Does that make me Diana Queen Bradford?"

He shook his head, swerved to avoid a pothole,
then glanced at her with a wicked grin. "You wish,"
he teased. "You do realize, don't you, that now that
you know my secret, I'm going to have to find a way
to silence you?"

Her mind zapped instantly to one of the more plea-
surable methods he might use to silence her and Diana found herself struggling to catch her breath. She
hadn't forgotten the way his kiss had felt, not for a
moment. Its very gentleness had set it apart from
every kiss she had ever received from any other man.

Not that there'd been all that many. An impatient

man, Jack had seldom bothered to kiss her. When he had, it had been an obvious part of his lovemaking routine. As foreplay, it had all the passion of a paint-by-numbers masterpiece.

Taking charge of her thoughts, she closed the door on the past. "King, hmm? You said the place doesn't have a name—have you ever considered calling your ranch the King Ranch?"

He chuckled. "I'm afraid somebody beat me to it. Have you ever considered calling yourself Lady Diana?"

"No, but when I was about five or six, I used to pretend I was a princess. It was a game my mother and I made up."

They fell silent again, but it was a surprisingly comfortable silence. When they passed a truck stop, Will turned off the highway and pulled up to the gas pumps. "Rest rooms are inside. I'll meet you there in five, and we'll stock up on junk food."

Feeling suddenly carefree and optimistic for no real reason, Diana stepped out and found herself unexpectedly surrounded by her husband's arms. Flushed, she said, "Careful with those promises, dude—I'm eating for two, remember?"

"I remember," he said, his voice a shade deeper, huskier than usual. She was still surrounded by his loose embrace, and just before he stepped away, he leaned down and placed his firm lips over hers.

And, just as it had before, the world tilted on its axis and trembled for an instant before righting itself again.

"Well," she said breathlessly, sidestepping his arms. "I'd better—that is, I really do have to, um, wash up."

Will didn't say a word, but he stood and watched as she scurried across the paved apron and let herself inside Taylor's Trux Top, Gas and Great Eats. First thing he needed to do was go online and check out the care and feeding of a pregnant female. An elusive, funny, increasingly fascinating pregnant female.

Less than an hour later, having made little conversation but great inroads in the popcorn, the fat-free corn chips and the bottled iced tea, Will turned off at a mailbox onto an unmarked road that was obviously well maintained. "Look, I'd better warn you, Miss Emma's going to want to fatten you up. In fact, once she finds out about the baby, she might not even allow you out of bed. Her husband, Tack Gilbert, manages the ranch, but Miss Emma runs the house with an iron hand."

"So what if we don't tell her?" Diana suggested. "About the baby, I mean?"

"Does it show yet?" He glanced at her flat stomach. "I didn't mean that, exactly, but is there some clue—something women pick up on that men don't?"

"Later there might be. Dark patches on my face." He looked so horrified that she burst out laughing. "What, you're going to divorce me if I get a few brown patches? What about stretch marks?"

Her smile faded as the implications struck them both. If she had stretch marks—and she probably would before it was over—he would never see them. They didn't have that kind of relationship.

And crazy or not, Diana found herself almost wishing they did.

Then she was staring at the house. From what he'd

said, about the ranch not having a name, she had expected a small frame house and a few unpainted outbuildings.

Rancho Anonymous was far more than that. The main house was built of log and cedar siding, with lots of stone and glass. There was a wraparound deck, part of it open, the rest roofed over. Perfect, she thought, for watching the sun go down over that pasture full of horses.

"Oh, my," she breathed. "I didn't know there was that much green grass out in the country."

Will pointed out the windmill and explained about the irrigation system. "Those hedgerows you see out there are all that keep the sand from covering it when we get a hard blow." Taking her arm, he led her toward the house. "Ranching's a hell of a lot more interesting than spreadsheets."

"I can imagine," she said, and she could. Funny thing—seeing him at work, she could never have imagined him on a ranch, looking as though he belonged. Yet, now that she'd seen him here, she had trouble picturing him back at work, soberly suited, addressing a meeting of the board.

"Is that an airport?" She pointed to a flat metal building in the distance with a wind sock on the roof.

"Just a hangar. I keep a couple of small planes here in case I need to get back to town in a hurry."

A couple of small planes. Uh-huh. It was just beginning to sink in that her husband was an extremely wealthy man. With Jack, it had showed. The house he'd lived in—the expensive toys with which he surrounded himself. He'd collected old cars. Bentleys. He'd once joked that while a Bentley wasn't quite as ostentatious as a Rolls, it was common knowledge that anyone who could afford a Bentley could easily afford a Rolls.

It hadn't been common knowledge to her. She'd never even heard of a Bentley. Will drove a luxury sedan, but she didn't think it was a Bentley, much less a Rolls. But at least it didn't have a gigantic pair of horns mounted on the hood. He owned two planes and probably one of those pickup trucks she saw over by one of the barns.

Her father had driven a battered old VW bug covered with faded hand-painted slogans. Flower Power. Make Love, Not War.

Feeling suddenly out of her depth, Diana glanced uncertainly at the man beside her. He dropped a casual arm across her shoulder and led her toward the house. "Come on inside and meet Emma. Tack can bring in our bags later."

She was no horsewoman. That much quickly became evident. Even though Will had put her up on the fattest, oldest, slowest mare in his stable, she clung to the reins and the saddle horn with both hands and tried to hook her legs around the creature's broad belly.

"You dig your toes in any deeper and she's going to take off with you," he warned. The manager, Tack, was grinning through his tobacco-stained handlebar moustache.

"Fat chance. Look, you wanted me to ride, I'm riding, okay? Can I help it if he doesn't feel like moving?"

"He's a she. Her name's Mairsy."

"You're kidding."

"No'm not. Some kid named her Mairsy Doats

before I ever got her. Actually, she sort of came with the ranch. Want to try something a bit more challenging?''

Diana looked at him as if he'd lost his mind. And then she tried to remember how Dale Evans had looked in all those old Saturday-morning movies. Petite and relaxed, for one thing—not gawky and scared half to death. A white hat and a fringed skirt probably wouldn't change anything where she was concerned. ''You know what? I sort of feel like lying down for a while.'' She wasn't above playing the pregnant female card. Might as well take advantage of it while she could.

''Sore butt, huh? Come on, then. We'll give it another shot tomorrow.''

She scowled at him. Sure they would. And the sun would rise in the west.

Miss Emma took everything in her stride. When Will had first introduced her as his wife, she'd looked startled, but quickly rallied. ''Well, now, I'd better put another pillow on the bed. Mr. Will uses both of 'em. You want one or two?''

Diana's mouth must have fallen open. Will had closed it for her with a thumb under her chin and said, ''Give us any extras you can round up, Emma. We'll work it out, all right?''

They had worked it out. The first night she had slept in the master bedroom while Will slept in the room across the hall. He'd been willing to share a room, but as he was pretty sure she wasn't ready for anything like that, he hadn't suggested it. If Emma had any question, he'd blame it on his snoring.

Which he didn't. Or at least, no one had ever complained.

Diana thought Will looked incredibly masculine in his ranch wear, which consisted of scuffed boots, a flannel shirt worn with a leather vest, and a pair of jeans that were worn thin and faded in all the strategic places. All he needed, she decided, was a white hat, and he could easily play the good guy in any Western.

It had been her decision to tell the housekeeper about her pregnancy. Will readily agreed. So they told both Gilberts over breakfast, allowing them to believe the baby was Will's.

"Lord bless you, honey, I know how that is. My oldest sister's been pregnant half her life. Raised seven young'uns, then helped raise two grandkids. Still looks young as ever, too, even with white hair. Claims it's all on account of the way she eats. Stuff I can't even pronounce. If beans and greens and good beefsteak aren't healthy, I don't know what is."

"That was easy," Diana remarked afterward.

And it had been, but after that, Emma insisted on coddling her, making her come in and rest when she'd rather be outside watching the horses or exploring the various outbuildings. Making her eat all her greens, which she truly didn't care for, and seeing that she had an afternoon nap.

"You take that girl up to bed, Mr. Will," she said as soon as Diana had washed up from her second horse-riding experience, which had gone only slightly better than the first.

Diana felt herself blushing. She rather thought Will might be blushing, too, but then, it could be just a result of coming into a warm kitchen after being out in a cold, blustery wind for hours.

"Come on, little mama, let's settle you down for a nap," he said, and she had no choice but to accompany him up the stairs.

"I might not know much about horses, but I do know how to take a nap," she grumbled. "I certainly don't need you to show me how."

"You sure of that?" Those incongruous dimples flashed in his cheeks. "You were pretty cocky when you climbed up on that mare today, too, weren't you?"

"It twitched. How did I know it was going to twitch before I could get settled?" Okay, so she'd made a tiny little noise. At least she hadn't fallen off.

"And besides," she said moments later when he opened the bedroom door and ushered her inside, "I'm hungry. I need something to tide me over until supper."

"I'll bring you up a snack."

"Oh, don't bother," she grumbled. "I hate crumbs in my bed."

"Seriously, as thin as you are now—"

"I'm slender, not thin!"

"Right. Well, as slender as you are now, you're still going to need to watch your weight. I went online last night after you turned in, and one of the things I learned was that—"

"I've never had a weight problem. As long as I exercise regularly and watch what I eat, I never will."

"Never?" he drawled, staring directly at the part of her body just below the braided leather belt. Making her entire body tingle with awareness. "Honey, pretty soon folks are going to start thinking you swallowed a watermelon seed."

She sighed, then grinned. "Look, what if we tell Emma that my restlessness keeps you awake and that's why we sleep in separate rooms? She was giving me a funny look this morning."

"What if we don't?" His voice was too quiet, his intent too clear. She could easily have avoided him, but instead, she stood there and let nature take its course.

The kiss started out as gently as the others had. Then Will tilted his head, bringing his hands up to clasp her face, and something changed. That tilting axis effect again. Feeling the tip of his tongue tracing the seam of her lips, she moaned softly in surrender.

Hot, wet satin. How could anything so soft feel so firm? He tasted of coffee and smelled of horses and leather and grain. Those long, hard muscles she had admired so much on their wedding night hardened still more as his hand dropped below her waist, cupped her bottom and pressed her even closer. Feeling his arousal stirring against her, she caught fire.

It's not the man, it's you, you fool! It's those crazy hormones of yours acting up again!

Whatever it was, she was suddenly more aroused than she had ever been in her life. The embarrassing dampness between her thighs, this fierce, mindless urgency....

Stop it before it's too late, a voice whispered.

Too late, too late, came the echo as Will eased her toward the bed. He was breathing as if he'd just chased down a herd of wild horses. On foot.

"I probably ought to sleep," she panted.

"You'll be sore. Let me at least give you a back rub."

She choked off a laugh. "It's not my back that aches."

His warm hand slid under her hips. "Here?" he suggested. "Or here?" he murmured when both hands came under her and he cupped her cheeks. "Or here?" His palms slid down her thighs and moved inside, where she was feeling the slightest bit of irritation from miles of walking and trying to ride that damned old plug.

Trouble was, she couldn't catch her breath to tell him to stop—to tell him that all she needed was a nap and a dusting of talc.

It wasn't true. What she needed was far more complicated and far more dangerous.

What she needed was him. This stranger she'd married. Needed him around her, beneath her, on top of her—inside her.

Later she never knew if it was her own frantic uncertainty or Will's common sense that came to the rescue. She only knew he drew away, leaving her feeling bereft. Deserted.

In a voice that sounded like a rusty hinge, he said, "Sorry. Why don't you sleep awhile? Maybe later I'll drive you down to my favorite watering hole."

She wanted to grab him by the shirttail and cry, Come back here, dammit, and finish what you started!

Which was a clear indication that pregnancy also affected the brain. So she rolled over onto her stomach and pretended to sleep.

Six

Will leaned against the door, eyes closed, and waited until his breathing returned to normal before going back downstairs. He didn't trust Emma not to see something that might not be obvious to someone else.

At least, he hoped to hell it wasn't obvious.

Nothing that pulling his shirttail out wouldn't take care of.

A simple case of lust, that's all it was. Lust shouldn't even be a problem when the woman he lusted after was his own wife…. What he needed was a long, cold shower followed by a long, hard ride.

He'd never thought of himself as a predator. They had a business agreement, that was all. He would look after her the way any decent man would under the circumstances. In this case marriage had seemed advisable just to prevent any awkward occurrences down the line. He was protecting the company name and coffers—not to mention one of his closest friends.

In Diana's case, her baby would have a father on the record, and she wouldn't have to worry about supporting them until she was on her feet again. No, not even then. He'd already made up his mind to ensure her future security. He had more money than he would ever need and no one to benefit from his years of hard work other than the few private charities he supported.

The one thing he hadn't bargained on was this "personal interest," for want of a better term. If he had to analyze it, he'd say it was comprised of equal parts of liking, respect and lust.

Lust alone would be bad enough, but combined with the rest, it was about as safe as nitroglycerine.

He was headed down the stairs when Tuck whispered loudly from below. "Hey, boss, are you awake? If you're done up there, how about riding some fence. Just got a call from Wiggins—he says some of our stock's broke into his west pasture."

Saved by the bell, he thought ruefully, collecting his hat and cell phone on the way out.

Supper that evening turned out to be a surprisingly enjoyable social event. Evidently, word had spread that Will Bradford had brought home a bride. Neighbors from miles away came bringing gifts of food, potted plants, whisky and two kittens that needed a home.

Diana leaned back in her chair at the supper table in the large, log-walled dining room with its massive rock fireplace, and thought, how remarkable—how truly astounding it was that even on a temporary basis, she was a part of all this. Her marriage might not be a real one, but there was nothing at all awkward later when the men migrated into the parlor while the women sat around the kitchen table, munching on leftovers and gossiping as they put away the food and dealt with the dishes.

Emma presided, after trying unsuccessfully to ease Diana into the position of hostess. There was no real hostessing to be done. All the women knew one another, and of the five, including Diana, three were pregnant. With the exception of Emma, it was a young group. Charlie and Wilma Wiggins were the nearest neighbors. Wilma, eight months along, with the broadest, warmest smile despite a serious overbite, leaned closer and patted Diana on the hand.

"Listen, honey, you might think you're sleepy now, but wait till you spend a few nights walking the floor with a colicky baby. Believe me, I've got two more at home, and not a one of 'em but what didn't wear me plumb out! See this patch of gray hair?" She grabbed a streak of white among the faded red curls. "This was Zac. And this?" She touched its counterpart at her left temple. "This was Zeb. Would you believe I'm only seventeen?" She rolled her eyes, and everyone laughed.

Talk turned to tomorrow's Valentine's Day play at the elementary school and moved swiftly through local politics and various ailments, pregnancy-related and otherwise. Everyone chimed in with a story of having to lose weight, cook for a husband with cholesterol problems or manage the inevitable heartburn of late pregnancy.

"Oh, honey, you haven't seen anything yet," said

Wilma as she scooped up one of the kittens and settled it on her lap. "You gonna keep 'em both, aren't you?"

"I'm not even sure if Will's apartment has a no-pets clause."

"Then move. No time like the honeymoon to get a man used to following orders."

There was a general outburst of laughter and scoffing remarks. Diana said, "Evidently, you don't know Will Bradford. He's the original immovable object." It was the sort of thing wives said about their men. Everyone knew they were only joking, still Diana felt as if she had just betrayed her marriage.

It was Emma who got her off the hook. "That man. I declare, him and Tack is a pair, all right." She handed Diana a yellow kitten and rose to turn off the sputtering coffeemaker. "Stubborn as a pair of rocks."

"Yes, but even rocks can be moved with the right equipment," one of the women—Gail, she thought—quipped. "Obviously, Diana's got the right equipment."

Everyone laughed. Diana blushed, and Emma glanced at her thoughtfully and said, "Why not leave them kittens here? We need a couple of good mousers."

And so it went until one of them men stuck his head inside the kitchen and said, "Honey, anytime you're ready." After that, there was a general shuffling as people collected coats and Emma and Diana cut several slices of cake and wrapped them to go.

"Go ahead, you better take it with you," Emma insisted. "We're headed into town tonight, too, me and Tack, and there's no point in leaving too much temptation in Diana's way.''

''Ask me, she's got more than enough temptation,'' said Debbie Truett, with a sly glance at Will, who had just stepped away to answer the phone.

Emma Gilbert put on a red wool coat and collected a shiny black purse. ''Tack's shut up the barn and I've started the dishwasher and locked the back door. We'll be back by the middle of the morning.''

This, as the housekeeper had informed her earlier, was their night on the town. Bingo, square dancing and a motel in honor of St. Valentine's Day.

Before the last of the taillights disappeared, Will joined her at the glass-topped front door. Slipping an arm around her waist, he said, ''Reminds me—I didn't get you a valentine.''

''Good, because I didn't get you one, either.'' She'd have been embarrassed to give him anything involving a mushy sentiment that didn't apply in their case.

''Had a good time, did you?'' he asked after a few moments passed in surprisingly comfortable silence. Both kittens had finally grown tired of chasing an empty spool and were curled up in a box, asleep.

As if she'd been doing it all her life, Diana leaned her head against his shoulder. ''I did. And you know what? It's the strangest thing, but I feel like I've known them all my life. They're all so nice.''

''Hmm. Did you have a good nap today?''

She could feel the heat rising to her face. At the advanced age of twenty-eight, with two or three boyfriends and one full-fledged affair behind her, she had no more control over such things than she'd had at fourteen. ''I slept like a log,'' she lied.

"Good. Because I'm afraid I'll need to head back to town first thing tomorrow. You might as well stay here—I'll be back as soon as I check out a few things at the office."

Lifting her head, she stared up at him. "Has something happened?"

"I'm not sure. Something's cropped up with the audit."

"Who called?"

"Jason Windover. He said Seb's kind of spooked, but he hated to interrupt our honeymoon. You remember Jason from our reception, don't you?"

"Dark curly hair, blue-green eyes and a terrific smile?"

Will's eyebrows climbed several degrees. "You noticed all that, hmm?"

"I noticed everyone there. Want me to describe them all to you?"

He grinned, and his arm tightened momentarily, then fell away. "Not particularly. Maybe I'd better warn you, they're all confirmed bachelors."

"So were you," she reminded him, and then wished she hadn't.

"Well, yeah…" He caught the tip of her nose between thumb and forefinger and tweaked it ever so gently. "In my case it was a TKO."

"A *what?*"

"A technical knockout. Don't you watch boxing?"

"The daughter of a couple of peaceniks watch boxing? Perish the thought."

But the irony of it had struck her long ago. Her father, a card-carrying member of the love generation, protesting for peace and eventually turning into an abusive husband and father.

She shuddered, and Will's arm tightened around her. "You're bushed. You need a glass of milk or something before we go up? Maybe another piece of that coconut cake? You've only had three slices."

What she needed was to delay the moment until she could align her defenses again. Tonight had been too pleasant, too relaxing. Too disarming. And with Emma and Tack gone, they were alone in the house.

"You go on upstairs. I want to make a couple of phone calls."

Forty-five minutes later Will replaced the phone and stared unseeingly at a photograph of Windrunner, an eight-year-old stallion, father of more than half the new crop of foals.

What the hell was going on? He'd left Eric to oversee the outside audit. Eric Chambers was young, but as vice president of accounting, he was more than up to the job. Odds were that he'd be taking over as CFO one of these days when Will himself decided to retire.

It hadn't been Eric who'd called, it had been Jason Windover. According to Jason, Eric—trying to convince himself nothing was wrong—had mentioned the discrepancy to Seb. Seb had put it down to inept auditors, but had confided his own growing unease to Jason, who, as a retired CIA agent had some experience with such matters.

"Look, Will, this doesn't involve me, but if you want my advice, you'll get back to town and check it out for yourself. We both know Seb has a few problems of his own to deal with at the moment. He might not be the most objective man when it comes to any mess Wescott left behind.''

It was common knowledge that Sebastian had never seen eye-to-eye with his father about much of anything, yet that hadn't stopped him from joining the family business. Now, along with trying to reconcile a mixture of grief, guilt and unresolved anger, he had his father's illegitimate son to deal with.

Will himself had taken measures to see that Diana's baby would never become that sort of problem. Seb might suspect, but he could never be sure, which was the best they could hope for, under the circumstance.

Whatever was going on at Wescott Oil, Seb didn't need anything else on his plate right now. After promising to fly in first thing in the morning, Will replaced the phone and spent the next half hour thinking over the possibilities. He knew damned well the books were in good shape. As chief financial officer, he ran a tight ship, everything documented and accounted for. If there was a blip on the radar screen, the only thing he could come up with was a mathematically challenged auditor.

While he was in town, he'd give Seb a call about another matter—maybe get his mind off the dark stuff and onto something lighter. Both he and Jason had a few reservations about Dorian Brady—hell, half brother or not, he was still a stranger. But they'd agreed tonight that if Seb wanted the guy inducted into the club, neither of them would stand in the way. No one else was apt to blackball him.

Standing, he flexed the stiff muscles of his back—it always took him a few days to switch from city mode to ranch mode. The two lifestyles used different sets of muscles.

By now Diana would be asleep, otherwise he might be tempted to talk it over with her. In which case one thing might lead to another…and then another…

He wasn't ready to broaden their relationship. His brain knew it. Hell, he had self-imposed rules about those things. Trouble was, his body was a slow learner. Good thing, he told himself, that underneath that elegant, understated beauty of hers lurked an iron will and a stubborn refusal to be taken over. He admired that in a woman.

However, whether or not she liked it, he was going to be looking after her for the next several months. Once the baby came they could renegotiate.

Earlier he'd gone online and found any number of interesting sites for pregnant women. One of the things he'd learned was that in the early months, and often right up to term, most women experienced an increased sexual interest. Again, something to do with hormones.

It had hit him like a ton of bricks. One minute he was studiously clicking away, reading about folic acid and calcium, physical and emotional changes, and the next, he was fully aroused. Libido fully engaged, and hell—he wasn't even pregnant.

His personal noninvolvement policy notwithstanding, he wanted her. Worse still, he was fast coming to suspect he might want more than just a sex partner. Which might be a problem, because once she no longer needed him it would be a case of, Thank you so much, sir, but now that Junior's six weeks old, I'm moving back to Pennsylvania and taking a position that offers day care, so toodle-oo. Been nice knowing you.

"When hell freezes over, lady," he muttered now. They'd both said a bunch of words in the Judge's office, and Will didn't recall any escape clauses.

Not that one couldn't be found. Hell, half the people he knew were divorced at least once. But that wasn't his idea of what marriage was all about. He'd had no control over what had happened to his first marriage, but this time he was here, on the scene. In control.

In the kitchen he poured himself a glass of milk, downed it in three gulps, then headed upstairs. Opening the master bedroom door, he waited for his eyes to adjust to the pale sliver of moonlight before approaching the bed.

She slept on her side with one fist curled under her chin. In the silence, he could hear the soft, puffy sound of each breath.

You don't know it yet, lady—hell, I just figured it out, myself. But this is it. You and me. Me and you and whoever that is taking up space inside your body. That makes a solid *us*.

A few minutes later, after a quick detour to the bathroom, he carefully lifted the covers and slid in behind her, easing up to her warmth. The puffing sound stopped, and he held his own breath.

Then it came again and he edged closer, fitting his body around hers and placing his arm carefully around her waist. Not a smart move, he thought, making no move to leave.

There was no need to set an alarm. He'd be awake at six, at which time he would ease out of bed without disturbing her—Diana. His wife. After leaving her a note, he'd grab a bowl of cereal and a pint of coffee and jog on out to the hangar. By eight-thirty he'd be in Royal, ready to tackle whatever the auditors thought they'd uncovered.

Diana opened her eyes. Something—a sound?—had disturbed her. She'd been a light sleeper ever since her mother's illness had been diagnosed, often lying awake for hours in the night, worrying, listening for sounds of distress—searching for answers.

Pregnancy didn't help. All those daytime naps...

Heat. Hot flashes were one thing, but the weight around her waist was no hot flash. Neither was the warm current of air that stirred the hair on top of her head.

Realization came instantly, and with it, a rush of arousal that was shocking in its intensity.

She knew the very moment he came awake. Felt his chest grow still, felt another part of his body come awake.

"Diana?" The sound barely registered on the black velvet silence.

"What are you doing here?" Her own whisper sounded harsh in the darkness.

"I didn't mean to wake you."

"Then why are you in my bed instead of your own?" She could hear her own heart. The more she listened, the harder it pounded—and the faster.

"Actually, I, uh—I needed to tell you something, but you were asleep."

"So tell me."

"I'm leaving early, but I should be back before dark."

"I already knew that. Not when you were coming

back, but we talked it over, remember?'' She tried
to be angry with him, but how could she possibly do
that when his arm was holding her cupped to his hard
body—when his breath was stirring against her hair.

When his arousal was moving against her with
alarming eagerness.

''If you're leaving, it's probably time for you to
get up,'' she said, shifting in an effort to escape his
seductive warmth. ''I'll just go back to sleep.''

His hand brushed the lower edges of her breast.
''Too early. Can't fly out until daylight.''

''Well, but can't you—''

''Nights are longer now. Longest night of the year,
in fact.'' They were both whispering, not that there
was anyone to overhear them.

''That's next week. I think. Will, this is going to
complicate our—our arrangement.''

''Our arrangement?'' His thumb and fingers cap-
tured her nipple and tweaked it gently. ''Don't you
mean our marriage?''

She flopped over onto her back and glared up at
the darkness. His warm palm, dislodged from her
breast, settled on her stomach. ''Our so-called marriage is a business arrangement,'' she whispered
fiercely. ''You know that—we both agreed to it, so
how could you possibly think I would…that I'd want
to—''

''Make love?'' He nuzzled her ear, sending chills
down her side. ''Don't you want to?''

How could she deny it when there was nothing on
earth she wanted more? Tomorrow would be time
enough for regrets.

Turning in his arms, she lifted her face to argue,
and that was all it took. A few hours ago he had

kissed her so thoroughly her toes had curled. Now he was going to kiss her again, and she was suddenly starved for the taste of his mouth. Some kisses were like Chinese food. It was impossible to get enough.

This time there were no gentle preliminaries. This time his mouth devoured hers until both of them were gasping for breath. Hot, sweet fire streaked through her loins, and her hands slipped over his sleek, hard shoulders, then moved down his chest to encounter his small, hard nipples. She could actually feel the shock waves echoing down his body, like a high-voltage current that affected everything within range.

She could have sworn he couldn't get any harder.

She was wrong. In the pale-gray light just beginning to filter through the window, she watched the planes of his face flatten out, watched his eyes darken as a grimace that almost resembled pain spread over his features. When his fingers trailed a lingering path up the inside of her thigh, she closed her eyes and whimpered with need.

Never in her entire life had she whimpered. With need, or anything else. Fragments of warning flickered in her mind like snowflakes, only to melt in the blinding, white-hot fire that threatened to consume her.

Please—oh, please...

Had she said it aloud?

Daring to take the lead, she shifted her position so that she could kiss his eyelids, each in turn, then his nose, that crooked, aggressive masculine blade of a nose. She kissed his chin, drawing her tongue lovingly along the angle of his jaw, then she buried her face in his neck, nibbling her way down the most sensitive trail to the hollow at the base of his throat.

He was groaning as if he were in great pain. "God, Diana, what are you doing to me? I'm only human," he whispered hoarsely.

"I'd noticed that," she murmured, heady with the unaccustomed feeling of power.

With one hand he threw off the covers. "You're not cold, are you?"

She laughed, a shaky sound that sounded different. Almost daring. "Do I feel cold?"

"Ah, Diana, Diana...what am I going to do with you?"

"I thought you knew. One of us probably ought to know what we're doing." She laughed softly again, trying to sound as if the earth wasn't shifting under her feet. She had never felt more unsure of herself, yet she couldn't have turned back now if her life depended on it.

His hands began a slow, incendiary journey of exploration. Fondling the sensitive slopes of her breast, he lowered his head to scour one nipple with a hot tongue.

A stifled sound escaped her, and her thighs quivered with the need to cradle his narrow hips.

"Not yet," he murmured at her small, instinctive movements. "You drove me quietly out of my head—now it's your turn." Matching actions to words, he proceeded to salute each needy part of her body, leaving kisses in each small hollow, tracing the crest of each separate curve with his lips, his tongue.

Her eyes widened, then closed tightly as molten lava flowed through her body, filling the valley of her desire. She pleaded with him incoherently. Bits of phrases—mostly sighs and whimpers.

Instead of mounting her, he took her hand and, one by one, kissed each finger. Then he nibbled the pad at the base of her thumb. His tongue traced a path across the hollow of her palm. Not until she was gasping for breath did he roll onto his back and lift her over him. Settling her astride his hips, he brought her down on him with exquisite slowness until her long, satiny legs were curled at his sides.

Somewhere along the way he had sensed that she had a thing about being in control. This much he could do for her, he thought—his last rational thought as the pressure built to unbearable levels.

Desperately he tried to hold back—to prolong the mind-shattering ecstasy, but it was too late. Far too late. Easier to hold back the sea, the rising sun....

In his last lucid moment he heard a cascade of sound. A soft, disbelieving *Oh, oh, oh!*

Seven

He left her sleeping—left with the feeling that something more was needed. That words that should have been spoken had gone unsaid. But even if he'd known the words, he wouldn't have spoken them.

Not this soon—not after mind-boggling sex. No lawyer in the world would accept words spoken under such circumstances. He was no lawyer, but even he knew the meaning of undue influence. Business was business, pleasure was pleasure, and trying to mix the two—trying to change the rules in the middle of the game—was asking for trouble.

Will made coffee, folded a slab of cheese into a slice of bread and let himself out, locking the door behind him. There was no crime in the area, unless a few straying horses and a broken fence could be considered crime. More a case of the grass-is-always-

greener, he thought wryly as he went over his pre-
flight checkup.

One of the skills he had cultivated over the years
was an ability to prioritize. Making a deliberate effort
to disconnect his emotions, he focused on the problem at hand.

The immediate problem, he amended. Unless he
misjudged the woman he'd left in his bed, that particular problem was going to require time, the patience of a saint and the tact of a diplomat.

A little while later, while circling over the Royal
Municipal Airport, he completed the disconnect,
knowing that the sooner he could find out what the
hell was going on at Wescott Oil, the sooner he could
get back to the ranch.

To Diana.

Hunger drove her downstairs. Diana showered and
dressed in record time, hoping Will hadn't yet left
so that she could settle things between them.

Praying he had, because she hadn't the slightest
idea what she was going to say. Thank you, I had a
lovely time, didn't quite seem to cover it.

He was gone, of course. It was half past ten. So
she made herself a hasty breakfast of half a cup of
whole-grain cereal with skim milk and three dried
apricots and a pint of coffee, to take out onto the
deck. Sooner or later she would have to cut back on
the caffeine, but not yet. Not when her whole life
had unexpectedly taken a dangerous new turn. A
woman needed a few vices to get her over the rough
patches.

She let the kittens outside, then she bundled up in
Will's flannel-lined denim jacket, sat out on the deck

and watched the steam rise from her coffee mug. It was going to take more than caffeine, she mused, to get her through this particular patch.

Of all the crazy things to do! It wasn't as if she was in love with the man.

Of course, she hadn't been in love with Jack, either, but at least she'd had a good excuse. Her mother's needs had come before all else.

How could she have allowed herself to think pregnancy was a good enough excuse? This was the twenty-first century. Wescott Oil paid well, the benefits were great—they even had child care. And single mothers were almost the norm these days. While it was far from an ideal situation, not every marriage was made in heaven. Her parents' marriage certainly hadn't been.

Nor was her own. Strictly speaking, it was a temporary legal arrangement between two consenting adults to provide for the security of a third party. Her baby. If Will hadn't rushed her—if he had allowed her more time to consider her options, she would never have taken such a drastic step.

And now, after last night, what should have been a straightforward business arrangement had become complicated beyond belief.

He probably considered it a quid pro quo. Damn all men.

Taking a sip of coffee, she burned her tongue and swore, more than the slight injury called for. She was still sitting on the deck, soaking up sun now that the morning chill had dissipated, when Tack and Emma drove up.

Diana rose to greet them. Tack headed for the barn while Emma came up onto the porch, her plump face oddly flushed. There was something about her smile that made Diana suspect that bingo wasn't all they'd played last night.

"Where's Mr. Will? Did you two make out all right for breakfast? I should have thought to make a sausage and cheese casserole and leave it in the refrigerator."

"We did fine." Diana collected her empty cereal bowl and coffee mug and followed the older woman inside. "Will had to leave first thing this morning. Something came up at work."

Emma shook her head and made a sound with her tongue and teeth. "That man. I declare, I don't know what it is with men and their work," she said as she took off her coat and reached for her apron. "Tack's just like him. Can't stand to be away from those horses of his more'n a few hours. You'd think they were his children, the way he frets about the least little sniffle."

"Yes, well. If you don't need me for anything, I think I'll take a walk. This is a lovely place to walk, much nicer than Royalty Park."

Emma took a roast large enough to feed a small army from the freezer and glanced at the kitchen clock, as if wondering if she had time to thaw and cook it for dinner.

"Uh...count me out," Diana said. "If Will's not back by noon, I think I'll drive back to town. I've still got some unpacking to do." And if Emma thought she was still in the process of moving in with Will, so be it. It was the literal truth—she did have some unpacking to do, including those old files of Jack's, which were probably of no use to anyone at this point.

Before Emma could argue, she hurried back to the bedroom and changed into her most comfortable sneakers, taking time while she was there to stuff her belongings back into her suitcase. She looked around at the room—at the bed—and sighed. She could have loved this place, but it was Will's home, not hers.

Striding out briskly for her walk, she followed the fence lines, pausing now and then to admire the horses. Quarter horses, Will had said, not that she would know one variety from another. She could tell a mule from a horse, and a cow from a mule. She knew from her brief experience that horses smelled like dried grass and manure, which, surprisingly enough, wasn't quiet as unpleasant as it sounded.

Maybe pregnancy affected her olfactory senses, as well as everything else.

One of the brown ones, more curious than the others, trotted over to the fence and blew its nose. Sort of a whuffling sound. It looked friendly, but Diana wasn't about to risk her fingers. "Nice horsey," she said.

The horse shook her head and backed away, and Diana continued down the dusty road. Walking always helped clear her mind. Exercise was more important now than ever. But even before she set out to walk her daily two miles, she knew what she had to do. If Will came back and she was still here, things would be awkward to say the least.

Dear heavens, they had made love and it had been the most splendid, mind-shattering thing she'd ever experienced! How could she go on living in the same apartment, working in the same office building with Will and not want to do it again? It would be like trying to walk lightly across a lake of quicksand.

It hadn't mattered with Jack—working with him days, sleeping with him nights. Every speck of feelings she'd had had been focused on her mother. With Jack she'd merely gone through the motions, and apparently that had been enough. He hadn't wanted more from her—although he'd told her once that her aloofness intrigued him.

With Will, aloofness wasn't even a remote possibility. She could just imagine going upstairs with him after the late news. What would they say, "Good night"? "See you in the morning"?

Or, "Shall we try for an encore...my bed or yours?"

The question was bound to arise, even if the words weren't actually spoken, and at the moment she wasn't prepared to deal with it. Her life was complicated enough as it was. Sleeping with a temporary husband—worse yet, falling in love with him— would only make matters worse. As long as she could hold on to her common sense and not get carried away by any romantic ideas, she stood a good chance of remaining in control.

"So that's what I'm going to do," she told Emma half an hour later, drinking a glass of tomato juice with a slice of lemon on the side. "I'll have to drive Will's car."

"I'll keep both kittens until you find out if you can keep them in town. When Will brings the plane back, he'll need some way to get back to town. Had you thought about that?" Clearly the woman was puzzled by more than their modes of transportation.

"What about the trucks? Couldn't he drive one of those back to Royal?" A week ago Diana couldn't have pictured him driving a dusty pickup truck. Now she could.

Now she could picture him in far too many ways for her own peace of mind.

"I reckon he could. Lord knows, we got enough of 'em around here. Next time you two come home, you can drive the car and he can bring the truck back, then everything'll be back in its rightful place."

Everything but her. Diana sighed. This was just one more indication of how inconvenient her life had become since she'd entered into a marriage of convenience.

She finished packing her suitcase, stripped the bed and offered to do a load of laundry, hoping Emma wouldn't take her up on it. She needed to be gone by the time Will got back. The next time she saw him she intended to have her armor in place and her arguments all lined up.

"We've done the honeymoon," she would say, "and it was lovely, it really was. But now I intend to go back to my own apartment. You see, if we stay together, I might want to make love again because it was the most...the most..."

She didn't know how to describe it, she only knew that if it happened again, some part of her that had remained untouched for twenty-eight years would be seriously threatened. And she simply couldn't afford to have that happen.

What was the slogan she'd seen once on a T-shirt? Life Is What Happens When You're Busy Making Plans.

Too true, she told herself as she braked at the end of the long drive, then turned off onto the highway. And, speaking of making plans, she would have to

go by the personnel office first thing in the morning
to find out where to report. The sooner she got her
life back on a nice, stress-free track, the better.

Something was wrong. Something was definitely
going on here, but for the life of him, Will couldn't
put his finger on who was involved and whether or
not it was deliberate.

Yeah…it was deliberate. Frowning at one of several computers in his private office, he wondered
what he had missed. He'd gone over every entry on
every single account until he'd practically memo-
rized the damned things. In a company the size of
Wescott Oil, that was a considerable feat.

Conclusion? Whoever had fiddled with the books
was either incredibly smart or incredibly lucky. Will
worked alone. For the time being he had to be sus-
picious of everyone with access. It had taken him all
day and half the night to home in on the trouble area.
Now he knew the accounts involved. All he had to
find out was how many of his employees had access,
narrow it down and go from there. He had a feeling
the trail might lead eventually to an offshore account.
Grand Cayman, perhaps—even Guam.

Eric was in the clear; it was Eric who had discovered the problem. On the other hand, knowing that
the discrepancy would soon be discovered by the
outside audit anyway, a smart crook might play innocent by pointing out the problem.

"Damn, damn, damn," Will swore tiredly. His
collar was open, his shirtsleeves rolled up. He
looked, as Tack was fond of saying, as if he'd been
rode hard and put away wet. Diana wasn't the only
one who was fond of old cowboy movies.

Diana...

He couldn't afford to be distracted until this mess was settled, but it was hard to keep the firewalls in place when he was so damned tired. God, he'd hated to leave her this morning. Every instinct he possessed had urged him to hold on to her—not to let her get her second wind and start thinking about what had happened. He had a feeling she'd been as stunned as he was at the intensity. Over the years he had slept with a number of women. Among them had been a few screamers, a yelper, even one or two groaners. Nothing had ever affected him like the startled symphony of notes that had cascaded over him when Diana had climaxed.

Even thinking about it now, he felt his body stir to life.

"Lady, you and I have some unfinished business once I get back to the ranch," he muttered. Reaching over his shoulder, he worked on a few of the knots at the back of his neck, wishing those in his head were as easy to reach.

He'd done about all he could do until he caught a few hours of sleep. Maybe tomorrow, with a fresh perspective, he could lay it all out so that it made sense.

Reaching for the phone on his desk, he let his hand fall back. Too late to call now. Emma would know that if he wasn't back by dark, he wouldn't be coming until tomorrow. He was too tired to fly, anyhow. What he wouldn't give, though, to stand under a shower until he ran out of hot water, then crawl into bed with Diana and hold her—just hold her in his arms. Absorb her warmth, her sweetness, the calm stoicism she'd shown in the face of what had to have been some pretty heavy stuff.

He still had a lot to learn about the woman he'd married, but one of the more endearing qualities he'd discovered was her ability to stand there with tears running down her face and calmly make the decisions that had to be made.

Unflappable. Yeah, that described her. Or maybe flappable on the surface, but deep inside, where it counted, she had her own north star.

Will's car stood out like a sore thumb in the parking lot behind Diana's apartment, but there was nothing she could do about it now. It was too late, and she was too tired to play car tag. Half her clothes were at his place, but she had enough to get by with.

First thing in the morning she would drive his car to his apartment and walk to work. Before she settled on her next move, she had to know where she would be working.

Awkward didn't begin to describe the situation she found herself in. Will wasn't going to like it, either. Him and his rule about mixing business with personal matters. Jack had had no such rules.

But she couldn't afford to think about Jack now. She refused to think about what Will would say when he found her working nine floors below, in a tiny cubicle.

She got out the iron and pressed a beige wraparound skirt and a darker tunic top, both of which would serve nicely as early maternity wear. Her hair, which she'd worn in a single braid at the ranch because Will liked it that way, would be twisted up on top of her head and anchored with a small clip and a few hairpins. If she was very careful, no one would guess how many butterflies were fluttering around in her stomach.

And if worse came to worst and there was no place for her at Wescott, she would look elsewhere for a job. It would have to be here in Royal, because she still had almost a month left on her lease. At the moment she'd be hard-pressed to come up with a security deposit on another place, much less a month's rent in advance.

After putting away the ironing board, she yawned, but was too keyed up to sleep. She was hungry, but too tense to risk eating. When Will got back to the ranch and discovered she'd left....

Well. She would think about that tomorrow.

Will sat in the rental he'd driven from the airport and studied the gunmetal-gray sedan occupying his parking space. He scratched his head and wondered, not for the first time, if he was headed for a premature mid-life crisis.

Headed for? Hell—he was in over his head. That car was supposed to be back at the ranch. If Tack had come to town, he'd have driven one of the trucks. Emma didn't drive at all. Which meant...

A few minutes later he unlocked the door of his spacious apartment. Adrenaline coursed though his body like water from a fire hose. "Diana?"

Silence.

"Dammit, Diana!"

She wasn't there. He knew it without even looking. The place felt empty in a way it never had before she'd come into his life.

He'd driven directly from the airport to the office.

This was the first time he'd been back since they'd left for the ranch three days ago. Still swearing, he tossed his coat onto the bed and headed for the bathroom. Leaning over, he splashed cold water over his face. He could have used a shower—felt as if he'd been living in the same clothes for a week, but it would have to wait.

He didn't take time to call the ranch to see if by chance she was still there, and someone who happened to drive the same model car he did had confiscated his parking place.

The lights were on in the third-floor apartment on the corner of Macauley and Spring Streets. Not bothering with the elevator, which was evidently one of Mr. Otis's early experimental models, he took the stairs two at a time, building a head of steam as he went.

He hadn't intended to pound on her door, but by the time he reached the third floor, he'd had it. Flat-out had all he could take.

The door opened. "I thought you might show up," she said quietly. "You could have called first."

Fist raised for another attack on the door, he was caught off guard. Couldn't think of a single thing to say.

"Do you want to come in for a few minutes? I can make coffee."

So he uttered the first dumb words that popped into his mind. "You drink too much coffee."

Well, hell, she was standing there in that awful place of hers, wearing what looked like a Polynesian circus tent, with her hair all wet and her eyes all pink-rimmed. Dignity, though. Oh, yeah—more dignity than a bucket of starch.

"Coffee would be nice." Even as he entered her lair, the weight of the past fourteen hours settled in on him, like a ton of bricks. After a quick glance around the room, he headed for the rump-sprung sofa with the fake fur throw.

"I'll just be a minute," she said.

He was asleep by the time Diana came back with a hand-painted tray bearing two mugs of coffee and a cream pitcher in the shape of a Holstein cow.

For a long time she stood gazing down at him—at the unshaven face with the incongruous creases that deepened into dimples when he laughed. At the shadows under his eyes and the touches of gray at his temples. How could any man look so exhausted, so distinguished and so sexy at the same time?

That was when it struck her that she loved this man.

Not just that she was in love with him. To her way of thinking, being *in* love was too often a temporary condition. Occasionally it might deepen into the real thing, but as often as not it faded once two people got to know each other and both stopped being on their best courting behavior.

Loving was different. It was a for-better-or-worse thing. Something that lasted even when both parties had aged beyond recognition. Something that encompassed all that had gone before as well as all that lay ahead.

She didn't know how she knew this—she simply did.

Being careful not to make a sound, she set the tray down on the painted footlocker that served as a coffee table, then lowered herself into a chair and waited to see if he would wake up. They had things to talk about—things to settle between them. He probably wasn't going to like her decision to move back to her own apartment.

Then again, he might like it just fine. After all, he'd been a bachelor most of his life. If he'd wanted to be a husband, he could have easily found a far more suitable wife. According to one of the women she'd met when she'd first gone to work at Wescott, he'd once been listed in some magazine as one of Texas's ten most eligible bachelors.

She could kiss him now and he would never know it. Did the sleeping beauty thing work in reverse? Would he wake up and fall instantly, irrevocably in love?

Or would she turn into a frog?

Eight

Without opening his eyes, Will came instantly awake. Sensing her presence, he tried to assemble his thoughts—his arguments. The spring that was stabbing him in the rump didn't help.

Neither did the smell of her soap and shampoo. The subtle scent of her skin. He knew her too well.

He didn't know her at all.

"Are you in there?" she whispered.

He slitted his eyes. "Am I in where?"

Diana shrugged and looked away. "It's just something my mother used to say when I'd close my eyes and try to shut out the—that is, try to pretend I was sleeping."

Interesting… "Is that coffee I smell?"

"It's probably cooled off by now. You were sleeping so hard I hated to wake you up, but I was afraid the rogue spring would get you."

He slid a hand beneath him, trying to hang on to the anger he'd brought with him. He had fully intended to remind her of a few pertinent facts, then haul her back and install her at his apartment until they could settle on some rules.

"Look, I thought we had a deal," he said. Tact and diplomacy was called for here. Not his long suit at the best of times, and this was hardly that.

"We sort of did, I guess."

"We *sort of did?* You *guess?* Try again, Diana." His wristwatch quietly signaled the hour. It had to be at least ten—maybe eleven. It felt like it had been a week since he'd left her in his bed back at the ranch.

"All right, we did. We agreed that your name will be on my baby's birth certificate, and by now everyone in Royal probably knows we're married. By the time my baby comes, people will have forgotten, if they ever knew about…well, about Jack and me."

"Uh-huh. Sure they will." Sitting up now, he gave her a curious look. "You really believe that, don't you? I don't know how things work where you came from, but I can guarantee that half the citizens of Royal will start counting on their fingers the day we deliver. The other half won't have to—they'll remember."

"Well, shoot!" she exclaimed indignantly. "Why bother to get married, then? And besides, I'm the one who's going to deliver. You don't have anything to do with it."

He studied her for several moments, trying to get a handle on her belligerence. He could have sworn it hadn't been there a moment ago. Wariness, maybe, but not belligerence. In fact, when he'd first opened his eyes, he'd seen something that looked almost like—

He must've been wrong. As tired as he was, mistakes were inevitable. "Correction," he said patiently. "We're both involved. That baby you call yours is going to be wearing my name when he comes into the world. That means I have a responsibility. And as long as you're carrying him, my responsibility extends to you, too. Are we clear on that much?"

She snatched up a mug of lukewarm black coffee, took a large swallow and grimaced. "All right, all right. Maybe I'm just not used to people who insist on taking responsibility. So here's what we'll do."

He figured he might as well listen. She had this thing about being in control. It wouldn't hurt to cut her some slack, just until he got to the bottom of this other matter. After that, well…they would see.

"I'll stay here at my place, you can stay in yours, that way things won't get, um, complicated."

"You mean you won't end up in my bed again."

He could practically hear the heat sizzle as it flooded her face. "That, too. It was just a—that is, we sort of—"

He took pity on her. They both knew what it was—a hell of a lot more than simple, no-strings-attached, mind-blowing sex. At the moment, though, she was spooked and he had too much on his mind to explore it in depth. "Sure, that's it. Propinquity."

"Pro…what?"

"Stuff happens when you're unexpectedly thrown into close contact. In our case, sex happened. We'll deal with it later."

"Or not. I've got plans all worked out. Long-term

and short-term. You've obviously got something on your mind, or you wouldn't have hurried back to town. So…'' She smiled, and it was almost convincing. "Why don't we each go our own way, accomplish whatever needs accomplishing, and maybe have lunch together from time to time so that people will know we're still friends?''

It was put in the form of a question, and he didn't have the heart to tell her it ranked right up there among the top-ten lousy ideas. "Still friends. Yeah. Okay, we'll give it a shot for a few days, then maybe we can have lunch and renegotiate.''

It was a weak shot across the bow to let her know that they weren't finished yet, not by any means. But for now he would have to set aside his personal problems and deal with something that involved several hundred employees directly, and peripherally, several thousand more.

The change of regime in the life of any big outfit was a critical period, even when the new CEO was a known factor. There were bound to be a few hold-your-breath situations right at first. Seb lacked his father's ruthlessness, but he was a damn good businessman. Besides, the board of directors would smooth over any rough patches.

On the other hand, the way the energy market had been fluctuating lately, if word leaked out of any past irregularities, things could spiral out of control before they could get a handle on it. The last thing they needed was a herd of stampeding stockholders.

Diana stood, looking oddly dignified in her colorful muumuu. "Go home, Will. You look worn out. Get a good night's sleep. If there's anything I can do, just call.''

He stood, bracing himself against swaying; he was that tired. "Thanks, Danny." She usually objected when he called her that. This time she looked as if she might cry. So he leaned over and placed a lopsided kiss on the side of her nose and escaped before she could throw him out.

What the devil, he wondered, had happened to his so-called people skills? He was no diplomat at the best of times, but normally he didn't go out of his way to make waves.

Left alone, Diana sat on the sofa, avoiding the middle cushion, and congratulated herself on taking control of her life. Just because she had wanted nothing so much as to throw herself into his arms and beg him to love her, that didn't mean she'd done it. No way had she surrendered a single speck of dignity. Just the opposite, in fact.

So why did she feel as if the world had just come to an end?

Sniffling, she felt for a tissue. She didn't have a tissue. In fact, the damned muumuu didn't even have a pocket. So she mopped her face with the hem of the short, full sleeve and thought with tear-stained amusement that her mother had been messy, too. It was evidently in her genes.

But as dearly as she'd loved her mother, Diana had never—at least not since she was ten years old—mistaken Lila Foster for a mature, responsible adult capable of directing her own life, much less her daughter's.

Even when he'd been there, her father had been worse than useless. He'd been vicious when he was drinking. When he was on drugs he tried to stay away rather than risk exposing them to that particular set of dangers. Which, she thought grudgingly, had been responsibility of a sort. The best Liam Foster could offer.

But it hadn't been enough. Not nearly enough. While he had never done more than threaten his daughter and slap her around, he had beaten his wife more times than Diana could recall while a terrified child had hidden under a quilt or in a closet and tried to find the courage to go for help.

It was a lose-lose situation. She hadn't even felt guilty at the relief she'd felt when he had piled up his van and had to be pried out with the Jaws of Life. Or in his case, the jaws of death.

By then she'd been fourteen, old enough to take control of her life. She had deliberately chosen the courses at high school that would pay off the quickest. Once her mother had got back on her feet emotionally, Diana had helped her go over the help-wanted ads. Fortunately, the economy had been in an upswing at the time. Diana had picked out a sedate new outfit for her mother and insisted she wear it to be interviewed.

Things had been good for the next few years, but gradually the past had begin to take its toll. Or so Diana had thought at the time. When Lila had lost interest in her job, as well as everything else, Diana had decided that it was their apartment, the same one they'd lived in for years, that was a constant reminder of the past.

That was when the moves had begun. Packing up all the posters and wall hangings, the linens and dishes and candles and pots and handwoven throws and whatever furniture they could cram into the rental trailer—most of it wasn't worth the cost of moving—they would find a new town and new jobs and start all over again. The pattern had repeated itself three times before they had reached the end of the line. Royal, Texas.

And now Diana was responsible for someone else.

Will stretched out his legs, tilted his chair and closed his eyes. For one brief moment Diana's face hovered on the fringes of his consciousness. Quickly he slammed the door shut before he could be tempted to linger there. All in all, it had been one hell of a day. He didn't need any distractions.

He thought about the way his ranch manager, Tack Gilbert, had been led kicking and screaming into the world of technology. Farm records, breeding records, sales records had all been kept in a series of dog-eared ledgers. "Who the devil needs one o' them machines when he's got pencil and paper?"

Who the devil, indeed. One of the reasons Jack's business affairs had taken so long to sort out was his insistence on his own paranoid brand of bookkeeping, backed up with scribbled records which he stashed away in places that had taken weeks to discover. A few transactions, Will suspected, had never been recorded at all.

All of which probably had nothing to do with the problem they were facing at the moment. Whoever he was, the modern-day pirate who had been smart enough to set up a string of phony accounts had excellent computer skills. He'd been savvy enough to wipe out his tracks so thoroughly that it had taken an outside expert to even get close to the truth.

Eric Chambers had given him the name of an ex-employee of the Department of Defense who could, in Eric's words, bleed a turnip bone dry.

"First the good news," the DOD expert had said after a marathon session that had left Will's office littered with chili-dog wrappers and cigar ashes. He was going to have to have the whole tenth floor fumigated. "I managed to follow the trail through four offshore banks and narrow it down to two separate accounts. The bad news is that I don't have a name for you. Whoever pulled it off was smart enough to wipe out most of the hard drive by overwriting it with zeros. That's a DOD method, if that gives you a clue. You might want to check your personnel files for a connection there. Maybe he got in a hurry, I don't know, but he didn't do a thorough enough job, which is the only reason I found out as much as I did."

"So that's where matters stand," Will had told Robert Cole a short time later. The two men had met at the gazebo in Royalty Park. It was about the most unlikely place Will could think of. He didn't trust whoever had milked Wescott Oil for an indecent amount of money not to have bugged his office, his apartment and for all he knew, the meeting rooms at the Cattleman's Club.

"I'll need to see the personnel files."

"My computer expert said you might want to look for DOD connections. Then again, geekdom prevails in some pretty strange places." Ordinarily, the first place he'd have looked was in his own department, but aside from Eric, he was no longer certain who he could trust.

"It could be a new hire or an older employee with a grudge. Lot of that going around lately."

"You show me a roughneck who's spent his life in the oil field who can make a computer sing soprano and I'll hand him the money, tax-free."

"Don't make any hasty promises. You'd be surprised the kind of people who take to computers like a bear to honey."

Will's temper, already on a short rein, tightened dangerously. He needed a shave, he needed a shower, he needed some food and about twenty-four hours of sleep. Even a couple hours would help.

He wasn't likely to get any of the above in the near future.

The shower, maybe…

"Don't make any rash promises," Robert had warned. "How many people know about the losses?"

"Eric, of course. He managed to stall the outside auditors until we can get a handle on it. Don't ask me how, because these guys are supposed to be hell on wheels."

"One of 'em's Eric's cousin on his mama's side."

Will stared at him, dumbfounded. "How the devil did you know that?"

Robert shrugged. "Hey, I'm a P.I. It's what we do. Impress the clients by coming up with irrelevant information."

"Which may be relevant in this case."

"I don't think so." Robert shook his head.

"Why not?"

Instead of answering, the young private investigator had shoved his hands in his pockets. Blue eyes twinkling, he'd changed the subject. "How's married life?"

"Keep your prying eyes off my marriage, okay?"

"So where's the bride? How does she like having her honeymoon interrupted by a little financial hanky-panky?"

"I left her at the ranch," Will said, but hell—this was Robert. The two men had been friends for years. "She drove herself back to town. At the moment we've agreed to put our relationship on hold until I can get a handle on this business at the company."

"Smart man. The way I hear it—not that I have any firsthand experience with wedded bliss, you understand—these things are tricky. Takes a man's full concentration."

"Which things, marriage or embezzlement?"

"Both," Robert had replied, grinning broadly.

"You got that right," Will muttered.

It was a few minutes past nine when Diana arrived at the Wescott Building the next morning. Not too early, not too late. Just right, in fact. Only the thing was, she didn't know where to report. She could just show up in the pool room, as the secretaries who worked there called it, or she could ask at personnel if she should report upstairs, and if so, to which particular office in which department. Maybe someone was going out on maternity leave and she could fill in until something else opened up.

After due consideration, she decided against just showing up in the pool room, where her cubicle was already occupied by someone else. It would be awkward at the very least. She had no idea how many people there knew she'd had an affair with Jack, but they probably all knew by now that she was married to the CFO. It would make a difference. She was hardly naive enough to believe it wouldn't.

Which was why she had a backup plan all ready in place. Not an ideal one, but any plan was better than none at all.

Twenty-five minutes later she sat in her car in the employees' parking lot and stared at the bug smears on her windshield. "I don't believe it," she said softly. She could not believe that Will would do such a thing. Had he deliberately set out to humiliate her? Presenting herself at the personnel office, she'd been offered smirking congratulations along with her severance pay. Severance pay!

"Well, we'll just see about that, boy-o," she muttered. Backing recklessly out of her slot, she came within inches of plowing down a fire hydrant.

The Royal Diner might look like a typical greasy spoon, but she hadn't lived in Royal long before she realized that everyone in town ate there at one time or another. At the moment, however, there was only one patron inside. It was too late for breakfast, too early for lunch.

Diana recognized the woman only in the way you would someone you'd seen several times but never spoken to. Passing the long Formica counter with the empty vinyl-covered bar stools and the row of booths, she headed for the door at the back with a sign that said, Office. No Smoking. And rapped sharply. She was still seething.

"Come in, come in, whatcha want, for Pete's sake, cantcha see I'm busy?" someone yelled from inside.

Anger was replaced by an impulse to flee, but before she could move, the door was opened and she was trapped. "Yeah?" said the woman with the neon-red hair and the cigarette dangling from the corner of her mouth.

Diana glanced quickly at the sign over the door, and the woman said, "Yeah, yeah, I know. Days like this don't count. You selling or collecting?"

"No—that is, I saw your sign on the window. The one that said Waitress Wanted?"

Six hours later she staggered into her apartment and collapsed on the sofa. Cursing the damned sprung spring, she shifted her position slightly, then leaned back and closed her eyes. Whoever thought being a waitress was easy work needed their head examined.

Slipping off her shoes, which had never been designed for waitressing, she rubbed her feet and thought longingly of easing them into a tub of hot salt water. Unfortunately, she didn't have a tub, only a shower.

Too much trouble. Just sitting would have to do for now.

The diner had indeed been in need of help. One waitress had left three days before to be married, another had called in sick that morning, and the one who had showed up for work had left with a severe case of cramps mere moments before Diana arrived.

Which was probably why the manager had handed Diana a clean apron, stuck a pad and pencil in her hand, and said, "You're hired. We'll do the paperwork later. Her over there." She'd nodded toward the sole patron. "See if she's ready yet to order. Been sitting there moping long enough to take root."

That's when Diana had learned that a waitress's duties included more than merely transporting food from kitchen to table and dirty dishes from table to kitchen.

The woman in the third booth was relatively new in town. She'd admitted as much when she'd placed an order for a Mexican omelet, a croissant and cappuccino. "I'm celebrating," she confided. "I just bought the flower shop—just now signed the final papers, in fact. Now I'm starting to have second thoughts." Her voice wavered, and her blue eyes looked suspiciously bright.

"You'll love it here," Diana said encouragingly. "I've been here less than a year, myself, but the people are so nice. What are you going to call your flower shop?" If the manager complained that she was wasting too much time listening to the customers, Diana might even rethink her impulsive decision to work here. She wasn't about to be rude to a woman who obviously needed reassurance.

"I haven't decided yet," said the woman, who had introduced herself as Rebecca Todman. And then she burst into tears. "Sorry. Don't mind me, I'm just—it's sort of an...an anniversary."

"Oh." Tears of joy? The poor woman didn't exactly look overcome with happiness. "Should I offer my congratulations?"

Rebecca had laughed through her tears. "Yes...maybe you should." And then she had told in starkest terms a story that made Diana feel incredibly fortunate by comparison.

"Hey, you! Bradford! This ain't no sorority party. If you're done over there, slice them pies, put 'em on plates and reload the pie case."

Several more customers had come in soon after that, and between keeping the dessert cases filled, taking and serving orders and clearing off tables, she hadn't had a single moment to sit, much less to think about her very first customer.

Did aspirin work on sore feet? she wondered just as someone began pounding on her door.

"Well...shoot," she muttered. In her stocking feet, she hobbled across the room and yanked the door open without bothering to ask who was there. The Lennox Apartments didn't run to security peep holes.

Will's fist was lifted to knock again, making Diana quip, "Déjà vu. We've got to stop meeting like this."

Nine

‹‹**Y**ou want to explain what you think you're doing?'' Will told himself it probably wasn't the most tactful approach, but she was his wife, dammit.

‹‹At the moment, I think I'm wondering which would suffer the most if I slammed the door—your nose or your fancy boots.''

He frowned down at his boots. They weren't fancy. They were plain custom-made boots, the kind any Texan who preferred comfort over flashiness might wear. Just to be on the safe side, he blocked the door open by placing a hand on it. ‹‹We need to talk.''

‹‹Like I said before, déjà vu. We've already talked, Will. I think we settled everything we need to settle. Unless you'd care to explain why you saw fit to blackball me at the office?''

‹‹Blackball! What the hell are you talking about?''

She turned away, and he followed her inside, noticing several things about her. Her hair, which always started out the day pinned up in a neat bundle on her head, was, as usual, responding to the laws of gravity. She was limping. "What happened to your feet?"

"I walked on them." She plopped down on the only decent chair in the room, leaving him the couch with the feral spring. "Why did you tell personnel I wouldn't be back?" she demanded.

"Because you won't. You know the rules."

"I know *your* rules. It's certainly not a company policy that employers and employees can't—that is they aren't allowed to—"

"Cohabit?"

"Yes, well we're not, are we? I live here. You live at your address."

"We're married, Danny." She looked so damned bushed he'd almost gotten over being furious with her.

"Don't call me that."

"Why not? You like it."

"When did I say that?" She was rubbing her left foot. Her ankles were swollen.

"You didn't have to say it, I saw the way you looked the first time I called you Danny. Like a little girl who'd been given a kitten and was hoping she'd get to keep it." He glanced around. "That reminds me, did you bring your cats home with you?"

"They're kittens, not cats, and they're more yours than mine. And no, I left them at *your* ranch."

"Did it ever occur to you that in your condition, you shouldn't be on your feet all day?" He'd come here mad enough to wring her dainty little neck, but one look at those sagging shoulders, the shadows under her eyes, and he'd lost his priming. How could he tell her that people were already talking about their hasty wedding? That there'd been whispers about the way she'd been whisked out of the secretarial pool to go upstairs and work for Jack? And now the rumor was, with Jack gone, she had set her sights on Jack's CFO.

Then, as if that weren't enough to set tongues wagging, she'd had to go and move out of his apartment and take a job at Royal's primary rumor mill—the diner. How the devil was he supposed to protect a woman who was so determined to self-destruct?

Summoning all the diplomacy at his command—which, at the moment, wasn't much—he said, "Honey, if you did it just to make a point, then you succeeded. Maybe I should have discussed it with you first, but—"

"Maybe? Just *maybe* you should have told me you intended to take control of my life? I don't remember anything in the wedding ceremony that gave you the right to tell me where I could or couldn't work."

She was on a roll now. Will leaned back and admired the glittering eyes, the pink cheeks, the thrust of her delicate jaw. He could have told her she didn't have what it took to threaten a man of his size, his age and his experience, but hell—he was a generous man. So he let her take the bit in her mouth and run with it for a little while. She obviously needed to vent.

When she'd gone on some more about being an adult, and about not needing anyone to tell her how to live her life, and that if she wanted to work at the

Royal Diner, there was nothing he could do about it, he figured it was time to reenter the conversation.

"Did the doctor say anything about stress being bad for a woman in your condition?" he asked in his mildest, most reasonable tone.

"Stress?"

"Yeah, you know—declarations of independence, shouting, threatening to break noses and toeses, issuing ultimatums?"

"I did not—" She clapped her hands to her cheeks. "I didn't...did I?"

"You did. What's the matter, didn't you get enough sleep last night?"

She glared at him. They both knew neither of them had gotten much sleep the night before.

"What did you eat today? You need to keep up your strength."

She paused. Knowing she could simmer down as quickly as she could come to a boil, he waited with every semblance of patience. It paid off.

With that quirky little half smile he'd come to look for, she admitted, "At least I got my exercise."

"At least? That means you didn't take time to eat. According to my sources, you worked your pretty little buns off on account of none of the other waitresses showed up for work today." Will levered himself carefully up from the sofa and stood, trying to look more benign than threatening. Threats didn't work. He'd learned that much. She just dug in her heels and defied him to do anything about it.

So he tried another approach. "Why don't I make you a fried egg sandwich while you change into something more comfortable?"

Oh, she was tempted, but Diana knew better than

to give an inch. "I'm perfectly comfortable," she lied. She'd worn tan, midheel pumps, her tan skirt and brown tunic top to the office that morning, then worked all day at the diner wearing the same clothes. The shoes were going to Goodwill first thing tomorrow. The rest smelled of fried food and onions, nothing a good dry cleaning couldn't take care of. But she knew better than to change into anything now that might signal capitulation. She needed every possible advantage she could muster.

"Fine. You, uh…do have eggs, don't you?"

"Nope." She smiled, loving the way he suddenly looked less sure of himself. As much as she hated to admit it, he looked almost as tired as she felt.

It occurred to her that he might be in some kind of trouble. Could the company be in trouble? It was being audited, but that was standard procedure under the circumstances…wasn't it?

If she were any sort of wife at all, she would sit him down, bring him a drink and say, "Now tell me all about your day, dear."

But she wasn't, and so she didn't. Not that she wasn't tempted, but she knew better than to yield control, even to that extent. "Look, I really, really would like to get a hot soak and go to bed. I'll eat something later, okay? I'll open a can of soup and eat the whole thing. I really don't need a baby-sitter."

"It's not the baby I'm concerned about, Danny—at least, not entirely."

"Will, I'm fine, just bone tired. I'm going to work tomorrow at seven for the breakfast shift. Carla will be back by then, so it won't be like it was today.

They're still hiring—maybe someone else will show up.''

"And you'll quit.'' It was a statement, not a question.

"No I won't. They're shorthanded, and I need the work.''

"The hell you do. No wife of mine—''

Knowing she had the upper hand, she smiled. The trick, she was learning, was to stand firm, not to give him any wiggle room. Whatever else he was, Will Bradford was a gentleman in the old-fashioned sense. He might rant and bluster, but he would never resort to violence the way a weaker man might.

"I hate you working there,'' he grumbled, looking tired and rumpled and entirely too lovable. Really, she was going to have to start building up her resistance against this man she'd married, or he'd be able to wrap her around his little finger.

"I know. And I'm sorry...your reputation and all—''

"Screw my reputation, it's you I'm worried about!''

"You know what they say—a woman's got to do what a woman's got to do.''

"Okay. All right...for now.'' He was still frowning, and she wanted nothing so much as to walk right into his arms and kiss away his frown, but they both knew where that would lead.

No way, José, she thought, echoing a Texasism her new boss at the diner was fond of using. But, oh, how she wished things could be different....

The next morning, dressed in a gray knit skirt, a navy sweater and her most comfortable walking shoes, she left for work at twenty minutes to seven. The Royal Diner was only five blocks from her apartment, which meant she could save gas, save wear and tear on her car and get a head start on her daily quota of exercise. The stop-and-go kind of walking she did at the diner hardly qualified, but after a day of it, she probably wouldn't be in the mood for anything more than a shower and bed.

The shoes helped. Or maybe the job just got easier with practice. Since Carla was back at work, Diana took time for a bowl of chili and a salad at eleven, before the lunch rush began. The morning sickness was gone, but she found that a small meal or a snack every four hours made her feel better.

By the time her shift was over, she didn't particularly feel like walking home. Her feet ached all the way up to her hips. Obviously secretaries and waitresses used different sets of muscles. So when she let herself out and came face-to-face with a scowling husband—her own—she was tempted to take him up on his offer of a ride home.

"Whose home, mine or yours?" she asked warily.

"Mine would be better. Big bathtub full of hot water instead of a cramped little shower?"

He knew exactly which buttons to push. Which was one more reason to resist. She'd gone down that route before. "At least in a shower I won't be in danger of falling asleep and drowning."

"I have a shower, too. I'll even throw in a lifeguard." His smile was guaranteed to wear down a marble statue.

They finally compromised. He would take her to her own apartment to shower and change, then pick her up at seven for dinner, with a promise to return her before his car turned into a pumpkin. "You drive a hard bargain, Cinderella."

"I do, don't I?" she murmured proudly. As tired as she was, she was learning to handle him. The promise of dinner was not without risk, especially if he took her to Claire's, known for its romantic atmosphere. But it was important that they maintain some semblance of friendship, even she realized that. What was it they called arrangements like theirs? Open marriages? Or was that when both parties were free to roam?

The thought of Will with another woman made her feel slightly ill, but no more than the thought of herself with another man.

"Seven," she said when he dropped her off at her apartment. "Shall I dress?" If he was taking her to Claire's, jeans and a sweatshirt would hardly do.

"Strictly casual," he said, and she yawned and let herself out. He didn't get out and open her door. He didn't hint that he'd like to come in for a cup of coffee. Instead, he smiled, waved and left her standing on the sidewalk.

"Well, shoot," she whispered. She waited until he'd turned the corner and then she limped to the front door and let herself inside the shabby lobby.

Not until she had showered and shampooed the smell of fried onions from her skin and hair and slipped on her favorite muumuu did it occur to her that something was different. Everything, so far as she could see, was just the same—same sofa with the tacky throw. Same slightly tilted platform rocker, a ten-dollar steal at the thrift shop. Same books on the shelf.

But not in the same order. The Dummy books had

been on the middle shelf, the romantic suspense on the top...hadn't they? She could have sworn she'd left the book she'd been reading on the sofa instead of the coffee table.

And those boxes...

Had they been stacked on the left or the right inside her mother's room?

It had to be one of the more bizarre symptoms of pregnancy, but suddenly she was almost certain someone had been inside her apartment. A quick search revealed nothing missing. Not that she'd had anything of value to steal. Even her mother's guitar was at Will's place, along with the watercolor, which was nice but hardly worth breaking in for.

She put it down to an attack of prenatal paranoia. That and the fact that with all the recent changes, her life seemed to be coming apart at the seams.

Will had said seven. She didn't know where he was taking her. Claire's was hardly casual, and she seriously doubted he would take her to the Royal Diner for dinner. The greasy-spoon special of the day had been country-fried steaks and hash browns. The very thought made her sick.

She wore her black slacks and a beige turtleneck sweater that came down far enough to cover the slight thickening of her waistline. She'd had to loop a rubber band through the buttonhole at her waistband and slip it over the button.

Will arrived at three minutes before seven. She opened the door and thought, This is a mistake. This is like giving a candy addict a big box of chocolates and saying, Look but don't taste. Sniff all you want to—admire the little swirls on top, but don't you dare sink a tooth into all that luscious, delectable sweetness!

He was wearing khakis that hugged his lean hips like a glove, with a black flannel shirt. Evidently he'd left his jacket in the car. His cuffs were turned back to reveal several inches of tanned, muscular forearm, lightly dusted with dark hair.

It's not fair, she told herself. He had married her out of some misguided sense of obligation, and they might even have been able to work out a reasonable arrangement, but then he'd had to go and make love to her. Dammit, it just wasn't fair!

She smiled, and he said, "Ready to ride?"

"Do I need a coat?"

"It's not cold. The sweater should be enough for the amount of time we'll be outside."

Not until they'd driven several blocks did she begin to wonder. She knew where most of the restaurants were, and they were not in this direction. "Will?"

"Salmon. You like grilled salmon?"

"Of course I like grilled salmon—who wouldn't?" She'd never had it, only the canned variety. "But where are we?" And then she knew, of course. He pulled into the parking lot and parked in his usual spot, under the security light, nosed up against the row of lush Leyland cypresses.

She could have argued, and he would probably have argued right back that this was a civilized arrangement for a couple who were married but lived apart. And then what? Tell him she was didn't trust herself alone with him?

He would want to know why, and the answer was just too humiliating:

I know you married me out of some misguided sense of honor and duty. Maybe it's a marine thing— you were both marines, you and my baby's father. But you see, the trouble is, I'm dangerously close to loving you. If I get any closer, I might not survive.

Sure. She could just tell him all that and wait for him to howl with laughter. And just before she died of humiliation, she might even manage to laugh, too.

"I need to be home by nine," she declared firmly. "I'm working first shift again."

His lips tightened, and she knew a brief moment of satisfaction at having scored a hit.

The salads were made, the table set for two. With candles. There was brown rice in a special cooker, and salmon fillets ready to go into something that looked more like an autoclave than a grill.

Fancy-schmancy. When she caught him sneaking a look at the instructions, she had to smile. If he wanted to impress her with his culinary skills, she could afford to let herself be impressed.

She wandered into the other room, avoiding the bedroom wing. An open door led to what appeared to be a home office. There was a mixture of fiction and dull-looking accounting books on the shelf, interspersed with several photographs. The kind of pictures Jack had displayed in his office, but without the same ostentation.

Will standing between two horses, a battered black Stetson on his head, a cast on his left leg and a huge grin on his face. Roy Rogers, he was not. There was another picture of Will and Tack leading a knobby-kneed foal from a barn. Slightly out of focus, but easily recognizable. The foal was obviously the center of interest.

She almost missed the third photo, as it was half-hidden behind a cigar box filled with loose change. Carefully lifting it out, she studied the face and the inscription.

"All my love forever, Shelly."

His first wife. She'd never heard her name—or maybe she had. Jack might have mentioned it, and she'd forgotten, but she knew as well as she knew her own name that this was the woman Will had loved enough to marry. A beautiful, starry-eyed face, a mop of blond curly hair.

No two women could be more different, she thought with a sinking feeling, than the first Mrs. Bradford and the second.

"Soup's on," Will called out from the kitchen.

Replacing the picture, she hurried into the dining room, a fixed smile on her face. "Smells great," she said. Suddenly, her appetite was gone.

"Actually, I was lying. There's no soup. What you see is what you get. I, uh, bought a cake from the bakery, but it looks pretty dry."

The conversation was stilted at first. She complimented him on the salmon, and he told her the grill came with a guarantee.

He told her he'd noticed her car was due for inspection, and she started to fire off at him but relented. He was a responsible man. It was his nature. At this point he probably wasn't going to change.

Besides, it was one of his more admirable qualities. He had a long list of those, a few of which could be threatening to a woman who was teetering on the edge of love and trying hard not to fall in and drown.

After the meal was over he served dessert. The

cake was indeed dry, but she ate every bite to postpone whatever came next.

She knew what she wanted to come next.

She also knew it wasn't going to happen. Once was enough.

Once was too much.

"I was looking at your bookshelf," she said. "The pictures—" They had never talked about his first wife, but there were rumors about her among the secretaries. The fact that no one had met her only added fuel to the fire.

Instead, she found herself telling him about the latest among her symptoms. Thinking things were in the wrong place, when they couldn't possibly be.

"You know how it is," she said, laughing at her own silliness. "You take things off a shelf to dust and put them back out of order but don't notice it until later."

"When's the last time you dusted your bookshelves?"

She sobered at that. "I don't remember. Mama used to…"

"Anything else you don't remember?"

"Well, how would I know if I don't remember? How often do you dust your shelves?"

"I have a housekeeper three days a week. I'm serious, Danny. That place of yours could be broken into with a paper clip."

"Who'd want to? It's not like I was hiding anything of value. You've seen the place—what would anyone want to steal? My new toaster?" She tried to laugh it off, but he was making her uneasy by taking it so seriously.

"You asked about my wife—"

She hadn't. She'd intended to but lost her nerve. "Shelly was killed when some kid broke into our place. God knows, we didn't have much to steal, but she ended up dead, anyway."

Dear Lord, she thought, appalled. "Will, I never knew—that is, I'm so sorry."

"Yeah, well…it was a long time ago. But Shelly wasn't thinking about break-ins, either, she was going about her business. And it happened. It…*happened.*"

What could she say? What could she do? "I'll get a stronger chain," she promised. The one she had wasn't even real brass. Even the screws were loose. She hardly ever remembered to use it.

"Stay here."

"Will, I can't do that."

"Dammit, things are going on at work, and I can't afford to be distracted by worrying about you staying alone in that dump."

"Thanks," she said dryly. "You can take me off your worry list."

"That's just it," he exclaimed, scraping his chair back so that it struck the fawn-colored wall. He raked a hand through his hair and stared out the window at the lights of the business district, only a mile or so away.

Diana stood, torn between offering comfort and escaping before things got out of hand. A quiet, civilized dinner conversation she could manage. Comforting a man who was tired, distraught and utterly irresistible was out of bounds.

Everything about him affected her. She knew how his skin felt—the resilient muscles, the silken hair on his chest that grew wiry below the belt. Her hands reached out before she could stop herself, and she must have made a sound because he turned.

"Danny..."

"No. I can't—don't ask that of me, Will. Please?"

"I'd better take you home," he said after a hollow moment of silence.

Neither of them spoke on the way. "Don't get out," she told him, knowing it would do no good to protest.

"I'll see you upstairs and look around, then I'll leave."

The truth was she wanted him to. Maybe not leave, but that was another matter. She had never felt threatened before, even though they had lived in some rough neighborhoods.

At least, not threatened by strangers.

"All clear," he said after a quick walk-through of her four rooms and bath. "See anything that doesn't look right?"

She shook her head. "It's all the way I left it. Empty milk glass on the table, shoes under the sofa." She tried to make a joke of it, but they both knew that not all the tension was due to the possibility of an intruder.

"Then I'll see you tomorrow."

"I'm working."

"I'll come for lunch," he said with a wintery smile.

She rolled her eyes. "Oh, God, as if there wasn't enough speculation."

And then, just as she thought she was safe, he turned and took her in his arms, kissing her so thoroughly her knees threatened to buckle.

''What was that for?'' she gasped when she could catch her breath.

''Luck? A down payment?'' He shrugged and opened the door. ''Hook the chain behind me, will you? You might want to shove a chair under the knob.''

''Now you're making me nervous,'' she said with a shaky laugh.

''Good. It'll do...for now.''

Ten

Diana paused outside the corner drugstore on the way to work the next morning after another largely sleepless night. Between her coffee habit and Will, she couldn't seem to fall asleep. What she needed was to start tapering off caffeine.

Better yet, start tapering off Will, she thought ruefully. Will might be good for her baby, but he certainly wasn't helping her peace of mind.

While she waited for the light to change, she considered going inside to buy liniment and a new set of shoe inserts. She was still contemplating when the light turned green. Maybe thick socks would help pad her insoles....

Deciding to give it another day, then pick up whatever she needed on the way home, she stepped off the curb. Instantly a car that had been idling at the curb picked up speed and raced toward her. Startled, she jumped back, but not soon enough. Something slammed into her hip, spinning her around as she fell.

"Oh, my God, did you see that?"

"He ran her down! He ran a damned red light!"

"Lady, are you all right?"

Of course she was all right, Diana thought calmly. She was simply lying there on the gritty sidewalk watching the fireworks display. But the dazzling lights quickly faded, and she realized in some corner of her brain that wasn't about to explode that they weren't real.

It actually happens, just like in books, she marveled with a disoriented sort of pride. She'd seen stars.

Slowly she became aware of the noise. The shouts, the cursing, screeching brakes and blowing horns. At least she could hear, which meant she probably wasn't dead yet. She seemed to be lying on her back with her head against the curb. She was still breathing. Dazed and terrified, but still alive.

Hands were reaching for her, touching her. Someone urged her to sit up and someone else said lie still until the ambulance crew could check her over. She tried to speak, to tell them that she was fine, just fine, but couldn't seem to coordinate her tongue and her brain, so she simply closed her eyes. Her head felt like a cantaloupe that had tumbled off a truck, but at least it seemed to be working. After a fashion.

"Did you see that idiot?"

"I called the ambulance! Lie still, lady."

"Call the cops— Ma'am, don't try to move, y'hear?"

She heard the voices. It was like dozing through an old movie—something that didn't really affect her personally. Breathing through her mouth, Diana opened her eyes, then closed them again. Looking up at the ring of concerned faces, she felt a sudden surge of nausea. *Not now! I don't want to be sick in public!*

"Shh, don't you worry, honey, you're going to be just fine," said a heavy woman with the face of an angel.

You're going to be just fine. Hold that thought, Princess Danny.

She was in a hospital bed. Her head hurt. Her arm hurt. Her everything hurt! "My husband—did anybody call...?"

"Yes, ma'am, he's on his way right now. He was in Houston when they got ahold of him, but I 'spect he'll be walking though that door most any minute now." The nurse adjusted her pillow.

"My baby?"

"Still doing just fine. You've got a goose egg—more like an ostrich egg—on back of your head, but other than that and a few scrapes and bruises, you checked out just fine. Doc Woodbury happened to be here when they brought you in. He called the clinic and had your chart sent over. He'll be by directly to talk to you."

She felt sick. Not morning sickness, but sort of the same. And her head really, really hurt, but pain medication wouldn't be good for the baby. Besides, she probably couldn't keep anything down, the way she felt now.

"Water?" she whispered.

"A sip." The nurse held the straw to her lips. She sipped and would have grabbed it for more, but her hands were shaking too hard.

And then Will was there, looking thunderous—looking so concerned she wanted to cry, but for once in her life the tears wouldn't come.

"Don't say anything," he said. "Don't try to talk," he said, and when the nurse left the room, he leaned over and kissed her on the mouth. Which was probably the only part of her that didn't actually hurt.

"Now you can talk." His smile was beautiful, but it didn't reach his eyes. Those were dark with concern.

Or anger?

No, it was concern. For her, she thought, and felt the tears clog her throat all over again. She swallowed hard, determined not to show weakness, and when the absurdity of that thought struck her, she had to choke back a giggle. "Emotions all over the place. Hormones strike again," she murmured drowsily.

Will hitched a chair closer and straddled it. "It was a clear case of hit and run. Several witnesses said you looked both ways and—"

"I always do."

"—and just as you stepped off, a car that had been idling at the curb pulled out, revved up and kept going, after it had knocked you down. If it had had time to pick up any speed, you'd have been—"

She reached blindly for his hand, managed to find it and gripped tightly. "Don't say it. I don't want to hear it. I obviously wasn't as careful as I thought I was being."

"Something on your mind?" He arched his brows, and she was tempted to pull her hand away, but she needed his strength. Just for now. Just until she got over this awful shakiness.

"I was considering whether to buy liniment and shoe liners before or after work. Did anybody think to call the diner and tell them I'd be late?"

He hooted with laughter. "Honey, I suspect they've already guessed as much. News like that takes about ten nanoseconds to make the rounds. Right now they're probably placing bets down at the diner as to how long it'll take before the damn fool will be hauled up on a charge of assault with a lethal weapon."

She sighed, aware of aches she hadn't felt a few minutes earlier. "I guess I wasn't paying attention. Could I have some more water? I hurt all over, but the nurse said nothing's broken and the baby's still doing fine."

Will lifted her bandaged head carefully and let her take a few sips of ice water from the straw. Every instinct he possessed urged him to sweep her up, blanket and all, and carry her off somewhere where nothing could ever hurt her again. If he'd needed a clue that he was edging over into no-man's land, this was it.

He'd talked to the doctor. He'd talked to the cops. The vehicle had been found abandoned about eight miles out of town. The guy it was registered to had reported it stolen a few hours earlier.

"They're going to keep you overnight for observation." He broke the news, hoping she wouldn't kick up a fuss. Holding up two fingers, he said, "How many?"

"Seventeen."

"Smart mouth."

She smiled, then winced, and he wondered how he was going to break the rest of the news—that he was taking her home with him and keeping her there for the next sixty or seventy years.

Correction—until he could sort out this mess at work, get things running on an even keel again—and then he just might retire. He considered asking her how she would like to live at the ranch permanently, but this wasn't the time.

He had already lined up a nurse to stay with her while he was at the office, but that, too, could wait until she was back in fighting trim. "Go to sleep, honey. I'm going to stay here awhile and read the paper. I'm supposed to wake you every three minutes—"

"Three days," she whispered.

"Whatever. Anyway, don't count on getting much rest."

She was already asleep. For a long time, he sat there and studied her, wondering abstractedly just what it was about this one woman that made him act so out of character.

He hadn't been obligated to marry her. There'd been a time when he and Jack had been as close as any brothers. They'd both been marines, although they'd served at different times. They'd both married young. Neither marriage had lasted long, for quite different reasons. Needing someone to head up the financial end of the business, Jack had brought him in when he'd first set out to build his empire. They'd built the empire—Will liked to think he'd had a large hand in it, but Jack had been the driving force. Gradually, though, the friendship had cooled, due in large part to Jack's increasing recklessness and corner cutting. Of an entirely different temperament, Will had nevertheless stayed on, doing his best to keep them out of trouble with the stockholders and various government agencies. It had been a challenge, and he'd always thrived on challenge.

The woman beside him, looking so heartbreakingly fragile, was the biggest challenge of all. One he had accepted without realizing what it was going to involve.

How the devil did a man make a woman fall in love with him?

She protested, just as he'd known she would, when, instead of turning off at her corner the next morning, he continued toward his own address. "I've hired a nurse to stay for as long as you need help. She's Emma's niece. You'll like her."

"I don't need any help. I'm stiff and sore, but I'm perfectly capable of looking after myself."

He went on as if she hadn't spoken. "Her name's Annie. If you don't like her, I'll get someone else."

"I told you, I don't need—"

"Shh, think of the baby. She got pretty shook up yesterday—you don't want her stress levels shooting into the red, do you?"

"Her what?"

He grinned as proudly as if he'd just won the calf-roping event. "I've been reading up on the care and feeding of mamas and unborn babies. Care to ask me a question?"

Instead of answering, she yawned. Which was better than taking a swing at him.

Inhaling a deep breath, he thought smugly, Round One to the Texas Tiger. Little Miss Muffet has finally met her match.

By the time he had her settled in his bedroom—

they'd argued about that, too, but he'd stood his ground—she was too exhausted to go another round. "Let her sleep for a while." He handed Annie a slip of paper with his cell phone number written on it. "Call me at this number the minute she wakes up."

"Will do, Will. Don't worry about a thing. If she's half as nice as Aunt Emma said she was, you're a real lucky man."

"Thanks, Annie. She is, and I am."

The first day Diana was too miserable to argue. Annie was quiet, Will was absent, so mostly she slept, waking only when Annie brought her something to eat, or helped her hobble to the bathroom.

She had a lot of time to think, and mostly she thought about Will and her baby. Thinking about the man she was dangerously close to loving only made her more miserable, so she tried not to think about him and thought instead about the baby she was carrying.

What if it turned out to be a girl and she looked like Sebastian? How would chestnut hair with red highlights and silver-gray eyes translate in a tiny baby girl?

She thought about how startled she'd been the first time she'd seen Dorian Brady and mistaken him for his half brother. Sebastian had been out of town, so when she'd seen a man she took to be Sebastian coming out of his office on a Sunday morning when no one was there, except for a few people who were working to clear out Jack's suite of offices, naturally she'd been surprised.

She'd said, "Sebastian? Mr. Wescott?"

And the man had turned and she'd seen that it

wasn't Sebastian, so she'd apologized and hurried on to records, where she'd been returning a stack of files.

He had watched her all the way down the hall—she could see his reflection in the plate glass window at the end. Probably thought she was flirting…or just a little bit nuts.

Her baby would be Dorian's half sibling, too. Which somehow wasn't as welcome a thought.

She hoped it was a little girl, but as long as she was healthy, who cared what she looked like? Toenail polish did wonders for self-esteem.

Two days later, when Diana could manage to hobble around without feeling as if her left hip was going to shatter, she took matters into her own hands. "Look, I need to be in my own place, and whatever Will told you, this is not my home, it's his. We had this agreement—" She broke off, too uncomfortable to explain their complex relationship.

"He's going to kick up a fuss," Annie warned. For all her loyalty to Will, she was inclined to side with the woman when it came to a battle between the sexes, having just gone through a bitter divorce herself.

"We both know what kind of man he is." The kind any woman would be lucky to have, but not as an object of charity. "He thinks it's his job to look after any woman he considers too weak to look after herself. And I'm not. I might be a little banged up—"

"A little! You're lucky to be able to get out of bed, much less pack up and go home."

The smile Diana gave her was strictly woman-to-woman. "Does that mean you'll help me?"

No such luck. "Uh-uh. I'll drive you out to the ranch and let Aunt Emma look after you, but Will would skin me alive if I took you anyplace else here in town. Wanna know what I think?"

Diana didn't, but she had an idea she was going to hear it, anyway.

"I think you're the luckiest woman alive for being married to a man like Will Bradford. Believe me, there aren't very many good guys left."

"I know," she said, and sighed. "Is there any more ice cream?"

It wasn't going to be easy. Will knew that much. But for the moment he had to take a chance she'd stay put. The doctor had said her soreness would probably get worse before it got better. He recommended water therapy—hot, but not too hot, which Will could provide.

In fact, he might just join her in the hot tub. The thing had come with the apartment, but it had gone largely unused. When it came to socializing—or even unwinding—a hot tub, even with the jets turned on full blast, wasn't his first choice. He'd tried it a couple of times and could hardly drag himself to bed afterward.

However, it might be just the thing for what ailed Diana. Maybe he'd have one installed at the ranch, he mused, smiling at the memory of Diana perched up on top of old Mairsy, hanging on for dear life.

With that thought in mind, Will had removed his tie by the time he reached the door of his apartment. First thing he'd do would be to give Annie the night off. He didn't need a nurse to supervise what he had in mind. But before he could open the door, his cell phone rang. He muttered a soft oath. Not now—I've got plans, he thought.

Jason had reported in, less than an hour ago. Seb was up to his ears, getting ready to take over. Eric was out of town—at least, so far as anyone knew. He hadn't come in to work today, which was odd, come to think of it. His secretary said he'd been complaining of hay fever.

"Bradford," he snapped, holding the phone in one hand, unbuttoning his shirt with the other. He glanced around for a glimpse of either Annie or Diana. Yesterday he had brought over some boxes from her old place and put them in the spare room. If she was up to going through them, that was a good sign she was up for something a bit more strenuous. If not, he'd just have to soak the resistance out of her, because one way or another, they were going to settle things between them.

"Jason?" A moment later his face turned ash gray. He lowered his voice and said, "You're sure. There's no chance of, uh, mistaken identity?"

Moments later he signed off. Eric wasn't suffering from hay fever. He wasn't suffering at all. Eric was dead, strangled in his own home.

"Will? Is that you?" The husky voice drifted down the hallway.

Schooling his face not to reveal his thoughts, Will headed for the spare room, where Diana was kneeling over a battered cardboard carton. Surrounding her were stacks of what appeared to be sheet music, notebooks—the kind kids used in school—and posters, unrolled and weighted down with books and several old records. The vinyl kind. Santana. Jimi Hendrix. Janis Joplin.

"Hi, honey," he said gently, setting aside for the moment the murder of a man he had worked with for the past four years. "Feeling better, are we?"

"I am. I'm not sure about you. You look like you have a headache."

He had a headache, a heartache—aches in a few other places that weren't about to find relief anytime soon. "What did you eat today?" he asked, hoping to divert her attention. She didn't need to hear what had happened—not yet. Not until they knew more.

"My, aren't we nosy? For breakfast I had chocolate-covered peanuts. Baby had whole-grain cereal and low-fat milk. For lunch I had a giant serving of tin roof sundae ice cream—baby had mozzarella and salsa on whole grain bread."

Still on her knees beside the sagging double bed, she was grinning up at him. Teasing him. As if she sensed something was wrong and was doing her best to distract him.

He could have told her that verbal distraction wouldn't cut it. God, what he wouldn't give to hold her until the world settled back on its axis. To lose himself in her warm, sweet depths. To keep her—to keep his precious new family together from now on.

Instead he lowered himself to the floor beside her, shoving aside a framed black-and-white photograph. She reached for it, studying it with a wistful look on her face. "My family portrait...or at least, the closest I'll ever have to one." She pointed out a small blond woman wearing the uniform of the day—bell-bottom jeans with what appeared to be embroidery trailing up the legs. At least she was wearing a blouse. A few of the women weren't. Most of the men weren't.

"That was Mama. This was my father." Another out-of-focus face, this one with a scraggly beard. He was holding what was obviously a pot pipe as if it were a trophy he was waving. They were in a muddy field that was crowded with tents and open-sided vans. Guitars, drums and bass fiddles abounded.

She stood, stretched and rubbed her hip, then sat down on the edge of the bed. "I think there might be a cousin there somewhere, but I never met him. By now he's probably a stodgy old businessman with a wife and family, living somewhere like Dubuque."

It hit him then, the loneliness behind her wistful words. Struck an echoing chord he'd kept buried for so long it had scarred over. "Want me to track him down for you?"

She shook her head, but he settled down beside her. Protectively, he told himself. She had no business crawling around on the floor after what had just recently happened to her.

Somehow her hand had found its way to his thigh and rested there, as easily as a tame bird. "Don't bother. I might not like him, and then where would I be?"

"Better the devil you know than the one you don't, huh?"

"At least you're not going to run me down in the street."

Frowning, he touched the knot on her head, which was smaller today, but still very much in evidence under the glossy mane of hair. Probably because her scalp was still sore, she had let it hang loose. It was tempting beyond his ability to resist.

So he stroked her hair, and from there it took only a small amount of pressure to ease her head over onto his shoulder. "Haven't you done enough work for one day?" he asked. "There's always tomorrow."

But was there? Will knew he owed it to her to tell her what had happened at the office. The embezzlement that had suddenly taken a drastic turn for the worst. But that could wait.

This couldn't. This had waited long enough.

If he'd needed a reminder of just how fleeting life was, the phone call from Jason had done it.

"Diana, Diana..." he whispered. He needed her. The need was there in his voice, and she turned to him and lifted her face.

It started with a kiss. They had kissed before, but there was something different about this kiss. Not the effect—that was inevitable. All he had to do was touch her, think about her, and every part of his body was on standby alert.

She was with him all the way, her eyes told him that much. As did the shuddering little breaths she took, long moments later, when they were lying side by side and his hands moved up to cup her breasts. Carefully, reverently, he lifted her shirt, unfastened the bra underneath and paid homage to her newly full breasts, with the proudly swollen nipples.

Dear heaven, she was beautiful to his eyes. If she'd protested he would have stopped. It might have killed him, but not for the world would he try to lead her into anything she wasn't ready for. This hadn't been a part of the bargain.

But she didn't protest, and Will didn't stop, despite his concern about her injuries and the baby. "I'll be careful,'' he promised, adding silently, Darling. Sweetheart. Love…

And carefully he led her to a place all true lovers knew. A place where there was no yesterday, no tomorrow, only now. Two pairs of eyes began to glow. Two pairs of lips parted, sighed and then gasped with pleasure as tentative touches grew bolder. Caresses more creative. Her hands were timid at first, then bolder. Will forced himself to hold back his own impatience.

''Does this…? May I…?'' she queried softly.

''Yesss!'' he rasped as her hands continued to explore his naked body. Please, please don't let me disgrace myself!

She delighted him with her earnest attentions. It was almost as if she'd never done such a thing before. Never taken the time to discover all the places on a man's body where a single touch could be explosive, incendiary.

Where a kiss could cause an instant conflagration.

''Wait…give me a minute.'' Gasping, he covered her roving hands with his own, stilling them until he could regain control. He had promised himself to go slow in deference to her delicate condition. If she didn't choose to play by the same rules, that might be a promise he'd have trouble keeping.

She was more than ready, and not afraid to let him know. Lying artlessly on her back, her full breasts gloriously flushed from his attentions, she smiled at him. ''Well, are we going to do it, or are we going to take it up with the board of directors first and form a study commission?''

He burst out laughing and swiftly moved over her, carefully spreading her thighs to accommodate his hips. It was another first for him. The laughter. Humor had never been a part of sex before. "Did anyone ever tell you you're impertinent?"

"No...ahh!" She closed her eyes and bit her lower lip as he moved inside with the ease of someone coming home. Almost before he started to move, the pulsating bands of pleasure began gathering tighter, closing in on them like a vibrant rainbow.

"Your hip—"

"Oh, yes...more, more! Yes, like that." Breathing in tiny gasps, she clutched his shoulders and began to rock to his rhythm.

Moments later, when the world exploded, Will collapsed on top of her, then rolled over onto his side, carrying her with him. Holding her tightly, he breathed in the essence of slightly musky linens, sex and some herbal shampoo.

And love, he thought, amazed at this thing that had taken him so completely off guard.

Dare he hope she felt the same way? Was it possible?

Only one way to find out. "Diana—Danny—I've got something to confess, and I want you to have patience. I'm not very good at this kind of thing. Not smooth. But that doesn't mean I'm not sincere." Lying naked against her nakedness, their damp bodies still entwined, he searched for the right way to tell her how he felt about her, and about their so-called marriage of convenience. If she was afraid of commitment...

"Oh, hell, I love you, okay?" he blurted.

He'd expected most any reaction but the one he got.

She laughed. Again. One of her arms flopped out,

knocking a tattered copy of *Mad Magazine* off the bedside table onto the floor. She howled.

Disgruntled, he said, "Well, it wasn't all that funny. At least, it wasn't meant to be funny."

Rolling back into his arms, Diana gazed up at him, eyes brimming with laughter. "Want to know what I think?" she asked, her husky voice teasing.

He was afraid to ask, but she told him anyway, whispering, "Oh, hell, I love you, too."

It was long after midnight when someone pounded on his door. He'd unplugged the house phones and left his cellular in the other room. They were lying in bed, damp from exertions, not the hot tub. That would come later, when they'd got their second wind.

"Wait right here. Don't move," he said, and she smiled drowsily.

"I couldn't if I tried."

It was Jason. The low-voiced conference was brief. "Seb and Rob Cole are looking into the murder. I've got my sources working on the money drain. The two things are connected."

"God, not now," he muttered, squelching a stab of guilt. But if things were going to break loose— and it had been inevitable—he'd as soon it waited until he'd had time to ease into this new phase of marriage. Like maybe the next fifty-odd years.

Will's shoulders sagged. "Evidence?"

Jason, looking older than his twenty-eight years, shook his head. "Give me a few days. A week, at most. Meanwhile, keep a close eye on your lady. I think maybe her accident might be connected to what's been going on."

The trouble was, Will did, too. The thought of anything happening to Diana made his blood run cold. "I know how to protect my own," he said grimly.

"You've got all the help you'll need. Once we get this wrapped up…"

"The sooner the better. Meanwhile, there are things I can do to make sure she's fully protected."

"She's worth it, man. You're the luckiest loser I ever met."

He was referring to the bet they had made concerning their bachelor status. "You got that right," Will said with a grim smile.

He saw Jason out, placed a call to a top notch security firm with twenty-four-hour service, then went back to the bedroom.

She was sleeping, smiling at her dreams.

Easing into bed beside her, Will gathered her into his arms and made a promise. You and me, love. You and me and our baby. Everything else will just have to wait till tomorrow.

* * * * *

Watch for the next installment of the

**TEXAS CATTLEMAN'S CLUB:
THE LAST BACHELOR**

*when private investigator Robert Cole
is on a mission to solve a murder
but instead finds himself falling for
Rebecca Todman, his lovely suspect, in*

*HER LONE STAR PROTECTOR
by Peggy Moreland*

*Coming to you from Silhouette Desire
in March 2002.*

And now for a sneak preview of

HER LONE STAR PROTECTOR,

please turn the page.

One

Mornings were usually quiet at the Texas Cattleman's Club. But on this particular morning, there was a different quality to the silence. A heaviness. A somberness. Yet, the air seemed to hold an electrical charge, as well. A sense of expectancy crackled through the club. One of impatience. A need for action.

A murder had been committed in Royal, the victim an employee of a member of the Texas Cattleman's Club, and what affected one club member affected them all.

Though usually empty at that time of day, the club's cigar lounge was almost filled to capacity, with members having dragged the heavy leather chairs into huddled groups of four and eight. The members' conversations were low, hushed, as they reviewed the facts of the case and speculated on the identity of the murderer.

In a far corner of the room, Sebastian Wescott sat with a group of his closest and most trusted friends. William Bradford, CFO and partner in Wescott Oil Enterprises. Keith Owens, owner of a computer software firm. Dorian Brady, Seb's half brother and an employee of Wescott Oil. CIA agent Jason Windover. And Rob Cole, private investigator.

Though all of the men were included in on the conversation, it was Rob and Jason whose expertise Seb sought in finding Eric Chambers's murderer.

Seb glanced at Jason. "I know that your participation on this case will have to remain unofficial, due to your status as a CIA agent, but I'd appreciate any assistance or advice you have to offer."

Jason tightened his lips and nodded. "You know I'll do everything I can."

Seb turned to Rob Cole. "The police, of course, are conducting their own investigation, but I want you on the case. I've already informed the police that they are to coordinate their efforts with yours."

Rob nodded, his mind moving automatically into investigative mode. "Brief me on what you know about the murder."

Seb dragged a weary hand down his face, but didn't come close to smoothing away the deep lines of tension that creased it. "Not much."

"Who found the body?"

"Rebecca Todman. New in town. A neighbor of Eric's. She owns a floral shop and, according to her, was hired by him to tend his plants."

Rob frowned as he studied Seb. "You don't believe her story?"

Seb shot to his feet, tossing up a hand. "Hell, I don't know who or what to believe!" He paced away a few steps, then stopped and rammed his hands in his pockets. He heaved a breath, then glanced back at Rob. "Sorry," he muttered. "I haven't had more than three straight hours of sleep in the past week, and when I arrived back at the office this morning, I had *this* dumped on me. The only thing I know for sure is that Eric is dead. And I want his murderer found."

"Okay," Rob agreed carefully, aware of the responsibility Seb assumed for all his employees. "Let's start at the beginning and review the facts."

Seb sat back down, more in control now, but a far cry from calm. "According to the police reports, the Todman woman found Eric this morning around eight when she went to water his plants. He'd been strangled with his own necktie."

Rob leaned forward, bracing his elbows on his knees. "Any sign of a break-in?"

"No."

"Robbery?"

"Not that the police have been able to determine."

"Any known enemies?"

"None that I'm aware of."

"How about women? Any disgruntled girlfriends in his past? A jealous husband maybe looking to get even?"

Seb lifted a brow. "Eric?" At Rob's nod, he snorted. "Hardly. I don't think Eric's ever had a girlfriend. Lived with his mother until she died a couple of years ago. The only woman in Eric's life is— was," he clarified, frowning, "a cat. Sadie. Treated her like she was human. Rushed home from work at lunch every day, just to check on her.'' He shook his head. ''No. Eric didn't have any jealous husbands gunning for him, and he didn't have any girlfriends, either. Just old Sadie.''

''What about this Todman woman?'' Rob pressed. ''Do you think she and Eric have been involved?''

Seb lifted a shoulder. ''Maybe. Though I doubt it. Eric was…well, he was a bit on the strange side. A loner who kept to himself. Very protective of his personal life. No,'' he said, his frown deepening, as he considered, ''More like secretive. Forget it,'' he said, waving away Rob's suggestion of a possible relationship. ''There was nothing between them. He was a lot older than her. And he was fussy, if you get what I mean. About the way he dressed. The way he kept his house and car. Lived his whole life on a time schedule, never deviating a minute or two one way or the other. Hell, a woman would have messed up his life too much for him to ever want one around. The guy was a confirmed bachelor.''

''Sounds like about 90 percent of the members of the Texas Cattleman's Club.''

Seb cut Rob a curious glance, then leaned back in his chair, chuckling. ''Yeah, it does. Though that number's dwindling fast. I'm beginning to wonder how we're going to decide how to fund the profits from the Texas Cattleman's Ball.''

''I thought the terms of the bet were that the last bachelor standing prior to the Ball got to choose which charity would receive the money?'' Jason interjected.

''True,'' Seb conceded. ''But since Will here is married now and out of the running, that only leaves four of us. Just makes me wonder how many more will fall before it's time for the Ball.''

Rob rose, preparing to leave. ''You can quit your worrying, because there'll be at least one.'' At Seb's questioning look, he tapped a finger against his chest. ''Me.''

* * * * *

You are invited to enter the exclusive, masculine world of the...

Silhouette Desire's powerful miniseries features five wealthy Texas bachelors—all members of the state's most prestigious club—who set out to uncover a traitor in their midst... and discover their true loves!

THE MILLIONAIRE'S PREGNANT BRIDE
by Dixie Browning
February 2002 (SD #1420)

HER LONE STAR PROTECTOR
by Peggy Moreland
March 2002 (SD #1426)

TALL, DARK...AND FRAMED?
by Cathleen Galitz
April 2002 (SD #1433)

THE PLAYBOY MEETS HIS MATCH
by Sara Orwig
May 2002 (SD #1438)

THE BACHELOR TAKES A WIFE
by Jackie Merritt
June 2002 (SD #1444)

Available at your favorite retail outlet.

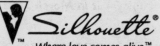

Where love comes alive™

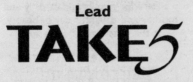

This Mother's Day
Give Your Mom
A Royal Treat

Win a fabulous one-week vacation in
Puerto Rico for you and your mother at
the luxurious Inter-Continental San Juan
Resort & Casino. The prize includes round
trip airfare for two, breakfast daily and a
mother and daughter day of beauty
at the beachfront hotel's spa.

INTER·CONTINENTAL
San Juan
RESORT & CASINO

Here's all you have to do:

Tell us in 100 words or less how your
mother helped with the romance in your
life. It may be a story about your engagement,
wedding or those boyfriends when you were
a teenager or any other romantic advice
from your mother. The entry will be judged
based on its originality, emotionally
compelling nature and sincerity.
See official rules on following page.

Send your entry to:
Mother's Day Contest

In Canada
P.O. Box 637
Fort Erie, Ontario
L2A 5X3

In U.S.A.
P.O. Box 9076
3010 Walden Ave.
Buffalo, NY
14269-9076

Or enter online at www.eHarlequin.com

Two ways to enter:

Via The Internet: Log on to the Harlequin romance website (www.eHarlequin.com) anytime beginning 12:01 a.m. E.S.T., January 1, 2002 through 11:59 p.m. E.S.T., April 1, 2002 and follow the directions displayed on-line to enter your name, address (including zip code), e-mail address and in 100 words or fewer, describe how your mother helped with the romance in your life.

Via Mail: Handprint (or type) on an 8 1/2" x 11" plain piece of paper, your name, address (including zip code) and e-mail address (if you have one), and in 100 words or fewer, describe how your mother helped with the romance in your life. Mail your entry via first-class mail to: Harlequin Mother's Day Contest 2216, (in the U.S.) P.O. Box 9076, Buffalo, NY 14269-9076; (in Canada) P.O. Box 637, Fort Erie, Ontario, Canada L2A 5X3.

For eligibility, entries must be submitted either through a completed Internet transmission or postmarked no later than 11:59 p.m. E.S.T., April 1, 2002 mail-in entries must be received by April 9, 2002). Limit one entry per person, household address and e-mail address. On-line and/or mailed entries received from persons residing in geographic areas in which entry is not permissible will be disqualified.

Entries will be judged by a panel of judges, consisting of members of the Harlequin editorial, marketing and public relations staff using the following criteria:
- Originality - 50%
- Emotional Appeal - 25%
- Sincerity - 25%

In the event of a tie, duplicate prizes will be awarded. Decisions of the judges are final.

Prize: A 6-night/7-day stay for two at the Inter-Continental San Juan Resort & Casino, including round-trip coach air transportation from gateway airport nearest winner's home (approximate retail value: $4,000). Prize includes breakfast daily and a mother and daughter day of beauty at the beachfront hotel's spa. Prize consists of only those items listed as part of the prize. Prize is valued in U.S. currency.

All entries become the property of Torstar Corp. and will not be returned. No responsibility is assumed for lost, late, illegible, incomplete, inaccurate, non-delivered or misdirected mail or misdirected e-mail, for technical, hardware or software failures of any kind, lost or unavailable network connections, or failed, incomplete, garbled or delayed computer transmission or any human error which may occur in the receipt or processing of the entries in this Contest.

Contest open only to residents of the U.S. (except Colorado) and Canada, who are 18 years of age or older and is void wherever prohibited by law; all applicable laws and regulations apply. Any litigation within the Province of Quebec respecting the conduct or organization of a publicity contest may be submitted to the Régie des alcools, des courses et des jeux for a ruling. Any litigation respecting the awarding of a prize may be submitted to the Régie des alcools, des courses et des jeux only for the purpose of helping the parties reach a settlement. Employees and immediate family members of Torstar Corp. and D.L. Blair, Inc., their affiliates, subsidiaries and all other agencies, entities and persons connected with the use, marketing or conduct of this Contest are not eligible to enter. Taxes on prize are the sole responsibility of winner. Acceptance of any prize offered constitutes permission to use winner's name, photograph or other likeness for the purposes of advertising, trade and promotion on behalf of Torstar Corp., its affiliates and subsidiaries without further compensation to the winner, unless prohibited by law.

Winner will be determined no later than April 15, 2002 and be notified by mail. Winner will be required to sign and return an Affidavit of Eligibility form within 15 days after winner notification. Non-compliance within that time period may result in disqualification and an alternate winner may be selected. Winner of trip must execute a Release of Liability prior to ticketing and must possess required travel documents (e.g. Passport, photo ID) where applicable. Travel must be completed within 12 months of selection and is subject to traveling companion completing and returning a Release of Liability prior to travel; and hotel and flight accommodations availability. Certain restrictions and blackout dates may apply. No substitution of prize permitted by winner. Torstar Corp. and D.L. Blair, Inc., their parents, affiliates, and subsidiaries are not responsible for errors in printing or electronic presentation of Contest, or entries. In the event of printing or other errors which may result in unintended prize values or duplication of prizes, all affected entries shall be null and void. If for any reason the Internet portion of the Contest is not capable of running as planned, including infection by computer virus, bugs, tampering, unauthorized intervention, fraud, technical failures, or any other causes beyond the control of Torstar Corp. which corrupt or affect the administration, secrecy, fairness, integrity or proper conduct of the Contest, Torstar Corp. reserves the right, at its sole discretion, to disqualify any individual who tampers with the entry process and to cancel, terminate, modify or suspend the Contest or the Internet portion thereof. In the event the Internet portion must be terminated a notice will be posted on the website and all entries received prior to termination will be judged in accordance with these rules. In the event of a dispute regarding an on-line entry, the entry will be deemed submitted by the authorized holder of the e-mail account submitted at the time of entry. Authorized account holder is defined as the natural person who is assigned to an e-mail address by an Internet access provider, on-line service provider or other organization that is responsible for arranging e-mail address for the domain associated with the submitted e-mail address. Torstar Corp. and/or D.L. Blair, Inc. assumes no responsibility for any computer injury or damage related to or resulting from accessing and/or downloading any sweepstakes material. Rules are subject to any requirements/limitations imposed by the FCC. Purchase or acceptance of a product offer does not improve your chances of winning.

For winner's name (available after May 1, 2002), send a self-addressed, stamped envelope to: Harlequin Mother's Day Contest Winners 2216, P.O. Box 4200 Blair, NE 68009-4200 or you may access the www.eHarlequin.com Web site through June 3, 2002.

Contest sponsored by Torstar Corp., P.O. Box 9042, Buffalo, NY 14269-9042.